I haven't lived
fourteen years for nothing.

Certain things in life are inevitable. Like when you don't know the answer, the teacher is bound to call on you. Or when you go to the store in your rattiest clothes, and you haven't washed your hair in a week because you've had the flu, you run into the cutest boy in the school.

It happens all the time. I haven't lived fourteen years for nothing.

But now that I was going to high school, I really didn't want to drag my past behind me. I wanted a fresh start, especially after my disastrous eighth-grade year.

**Other Apple Paperbacks
you will enjoy:**

FOURTEEN AND HOLDING

Candice F. Ransom

AN
APPLE
PAPERBACK

SCHOLASTIC INC.
New York Toronto London Auckland Sydney

Scholastic Books are available at special discounts for quantity purchases for use as premiums, promotional items, retail sales through specialty market outlets, etc. For details contact: Special Sales Manager, Scholastic Inc., 730 Broadway, New York, NY 10003.

ISBN 0-590-40501-2

12 11 10 9 8 7 6 5 4 3 2 1   7 8 9/8 0 1 2/9

Printed in the U.S.A.   01

First Scholastic printing, July 1987

*For Frank, who married me
knowing I had flunked home ec.
And with apologies to W.T. Woodson High,
actually a very fine school.*

Chapter 1

Certain things in life are inevitable. Like when you don't know the answer, the teacher is bound to call on you. Or when you go to the store in your rattiest clothes, and you haven't washed your hair in a week because you've had the flu, you run into the cutest boy in school.

It happens all the time. I know. I haven't lived fourteen years for nothing.

So it was inevitable that on the first day of my freshman year at W.T. Woodson, I woke up to discover a pimple on my forehead. Not any ordinary bump, either, but a great big shining red zit in the exact center of my forehead.

"Oh, no!" I flew from the bathroom out to the kitchen where my mother was blearily cooking my father's breakfast.

"Look at my face!" I cried as I yanked open the refrigerator. "I've got to put something on it right away!" I began jerking bottles and jars out of the refrigerator. "Ice is supposed to make the swelling go down. And I read in *Seventeen* that lemon juice will take the redness out."

"If you add a little sugar you'll have lemonade," my father said, in what I thought was a poor attempt at humor, considering my whole high school future was at stake.

"Very funny. We don't have any *lemons*!" I shrieked. "Mom, what'll I do! Today is my first day of high school! I look like I'm wearing a miner's lamp!"

My mother set a plate of eggs and toast in front of my father. "Kobie, put that stuff back in the refrigerator before somebody trips. Let me see your face." She tilted my chin up to the light. "Why don't you dab a little of my foundation on that bump? That'll cut the glare, at least."

"You could always wear a paper bag over your head," my father suggested.

"Easy for *you* to talk," I said scornfully. "You don't have to go to work looking like a radio tower!"

"Kobie, don't go overboard," my mother warned. "What do you want for breakfast?"

"A Coke float. I'll fix it myself."

"Coke for breakfast? Do you want a *face* full of bumps?"

2

"It hardly matters now," I said, swinging on the refrigerator door. "I look awful, anyway."

"Eat something nutritious," my mother insisted.

"This *is* nutritious," I said, pouring soda into a tall glass. "Coke has lots of tiny little good-health bubbles. See? And everybody knows ice cream is loaded with vitamins." I added two ice cubes to tame the fizz and a scoop of vanilla ice cream.

My mother shook her head as if I were completely beyond hope.

As I carried my breakfast drink back to my room, I heard her ask my father, "What am I going to do with that girl?"

"Well, she *is* in high school now," my father replied in a dubious tone.

In my room, I put a stack of 45's on my record player and got dressed. My first-day-of-school outfit was a far cry from the Ugliest Dress in the World I had had to wear on the first day of school the year before. The gray-blue corduroy miniskirt and matching Oxford cloth long-sleeved shirt was a little warm for September in Virginia — to be truthful, *cellophane* would have been cooler — but it was my best outfit. I was determined to make a good impression.

Next I struggled into the white vinyl boots my mother had ordered from Alden's catalog. They were the cheap kind without a side zipper, and they were also a size too small, which meant I needed the assistance of a front-end loader to get them on.

The ice cream in my Coke float had melted into a grayish scum, just the way I liked it. I finished my drink, then went into the bathroom to work on my face. First I covered Mt. Rushmore with a Band-Aid, but that only drew attention to my forehead. I removed the Band-Aid and liberally applied my mother's Max Factor pancake makeup stick over the pimple. That cut the glare, all right. It looked like someone had lobbed a wad of clay at my forehead.

I wiped off the excess with toilet paper, combed my bangs over the spot, and practiced confident, there's-nothing-wrong-with-*my*-face expressions. When I had arranged my features into a mask of cool indifference, I collected my lunch money and my notebook, and headed out the door.

"Aren't you going to give me a kiss?" my mother asked, coming in from the kitchen. My father had already left for his job as foreman of the Grounds Department for Fairfax County schools. My mother looked a little sad, although I thought she'd be overjoyed to have me out of the house at last. All summer long she'd hovered around the calendar, counting the days till

September, and now she looked as if she had lost her best friend.

"Give me a kiss good-bye," she said again, as if I were going to Alaska.

"Mo-ther! I'm in *high* school!"

"You're never too old to kiss your mama."

I could see this was going to be one of my mother's difficult days. I pecked her cheek.

"My little girl's growing up," she said, standing back to look at me.

"Your little girl is going to miss the bus if she doesn't hurry." Actually, I didn't want my mother to notice I had helped myself to her eyebrow pencil while I was doctoring my face.

I waved to her as I went out the door, feeling a little like Stanley going off to search for Dr. Livingstone. Woodson High, here comes Kobie Roberts!

The bus was late and jam-packed. I found Gretchen shoehorned in the backseat beside J.C. Brown — she hadn't been able to get our usual seat, third from the front on the right.

"I was lucky to get a seat at all," she told me. "J.C., move and let Kobie sit down."

J.C. stared at me insolently. "Why should I?"

"Because she's a girl," Gretchen said, as if that fact wasn't immediately discernible. "You're supposed to give up seats for girls."

I leaned down and said in his ear, "J.C., if you don't get up and let me have that seat, I'll tell everybody in Woodson that you once wet your pants on the playground and lined your shorts with an old Popsicle wrapper so the teacher wouldn't find out."

He got up. Nothing like the power of blackmail to make a boy suddenly realize he's a gentleman, after all.

"I'm glad Woodson is so big," J.C. said as we changed places, "so I won't have to look at your mug, Kobie Roberts."

"Don't do me any favors." I sat down next to Gretchen.

Yet I could see J.C.'s point. I knew every single kid on the bus and had known them since first grade. We had all been together nearly nine years: six years at Centreville Elementary, then two years at Robert Frost Intermediate, and now we were starting high school. We knew who threw up on her third-grade teacher's shoes, knew who forgot his lines in the fourth-grade Christmas pageant and shouted them out when the play was over and the curtain was coming down, knew who got sent to the principal's office for popping milk cartons. Not to mention the Popsicle-wrapper incident.

At first it had been hard getting used to junior high, because our little Centreville group was only one of several grammar schools dumped into Frost. I felt lost and outnumbered. But now that I was going to high school, I really didn't want to drag my past behind me. I wanted a fresh start, especially after my disastrous eighth-grade year.

At least this year I had a few decent outfits to wear and also I was a whole year smarter. The only problem was that Gretchen wasn't going to high school with me.

Gretchen Farris has been my best friend since second grade. That year we were in different rooms, but because both second-grade classes had recess at the same time, we had noticed each other on the playground. One day our teachers made all the second-grade girls play "Ring Around the Rosie," or something equally cutesy and nauseating, while the second-grade boys got to have fun and kill one another on the monkey bars.

Gretchen and I were on opposite sides of the big circle. I was holding hands with Deborah Clark, a pale red-haired girl, and Laurie Allen, the teacher's pet. We skipped around the circle, singing that stupid song until the line, "Ashes, ashes, we all fall DOWN!" Instead of dropping to the pavement like a normal person, Deborah Clark keeled over like she'd been poleaxed, dragging me and Laurie Allen over on top of her. While I was struggling to get up, a puff of wind blew my dress over my head and everybody on the whole playground saw my slip.

I was mortified. It was bad enough being a puny little second-grader without being subjected to idiotic games like "Ring Around the Rosie." When I finally got my dress back down where it belonged, I looked up and saw Gretchen watching me. She wasn't laughing like the others, but staring at me as if she knew exactly how I felt. Life was *not* a pocketful of posies, she seemed to be agreeing with me. I think we were destined to be friends from that moment on.

In third grade, we were put in the same class with desks next to each other. I was sent out in the hall forty-two times for talking in class. I had never had a friend like Gretchen before. She laughed at my jokes and thought all my ideas were great. We were in the same classes through elementary school until junior high, where we were separated and my life became one continuous misery. But my miseries were nothing compared to Gretchen's.

The year before, in eighth grade, she was in an automobile accident. She wasn't wearing her seat belt and her head went through the windshield. Gretchen had to stay in the hospital a long time. The deep cut over her eye left an ugly jagged scar. Even after Gretchen was well enough to come back to school, she couldn't take the kids staring at her and asking questions, so she studied at home with a tutor. Even so, she had missed too much time and had to repeat the eighth grade. This summer she'd had plastic surgery and, although the scar was still red, it looked a lot better. In time, her doctor promised, the scar would barely be noticeable.

Today she had on a new outfit, too, and her strawberry-blonde hair had been cut to cover most of her scar. She had also gotten new stylish tortoiseshell glasses to replace the clunky black-framed ones she had worn to help hide the scar. The new glasses and haircut made her look smart and vivacious. Over the summer she had gotten even curvier, while I still resembled a coatrack. No wonder J.C. had been so reluctant to give up his seat beside her. In fact, a lot of the boys were eyeing Gretchen with interest. Nobody looked at me twice, but that was nothing new.

"Are you nervous?" Gretchen asked me.

"A little," I said. "What about you?"

Repeating a grade was a bad break, but being held back from high school another year was especially hard.

"I'm dreading it," she confessed. "Being in the same classes with all those kids who were seventh-graders last year. Yuck! Plus I've got a really tough schedule. I'm taking two extra classes, so I won't have so much to take in summer school." Gretchen wanted to catch up to me so we'd both be sophomores next year.

"You'll ace it," I told her. "You've already had most of that stuff once. It'll be a lot easier the second time around."

"Maybe. But I'll be with all those little kids! Except for you, I won't have any friends!" she moaned.

I wouldn't have any friends either, and it had nothing to do with being left back. Last year when Gretchen was out sick, I discovered that I had some sort of fatal flaw that kept the cool, neat kids away from me in droves. I only attracted one boy, if you could call him that — Stuart Buckley, who came up to my chin and who slammed my locker on my hand every day. With all her troubles, Gretchen had had *two* guys falling over her last year.

"We'll sit together on the bus every morning," I said. The junior high and high school kids from Centreville and Willow Springs, where Gretchen and I lived, rode the same bus in the mornings. In the afternoons, Gretchen's school let out earlier, so we would take different buses home.

Gretchen glanced out the window and saw we were just passing Weber Tire Company. She clutched my arm. "Oh, Kobie, we're halfway there! All I have to live for are these bus rides, and they aren't long enough."

I had never seen Gretchen so edgy. Usually, she took everything in stride. At the beach that summer, where our families shared a house, we spent a lot of time reassuring each other that even though we would be separated, we'd still be best friends. But maybe Gretchen needed more than reassurance.

"Listen, Gretch, I want you to make friends at Frost."

She turned toward me, her blue eyes round with disbelief. "I can't believe what I'm hearing, Kobie. Last year you practically foamed at the mouth if anybody else talked to me. Remember Julia and Midge? You were so jealous of them."

I fidgeted uncomfortably. "I know. But that was *last year*. I think we both ought to have other friends, just to help us get through this year."

"Do you really mean that?"

"Yeah, I do. Not only that, but I think we ought to make the *right* kind of friends."

I was sticking my neck out here. Gretchen had the ability to make the *right* kind of friends instantly — everybody liked her — but I couldn't make the *right* kind of friends even if I advertised in *The Washington Post* and offered a hundred-dollar reward.

"And how are we going to do that?" Gretchen asked. I couldn't believe her modesty. All she had to do was stand on a street corner for two minutes and people would flock to her. I was the one who had to round up friends at spear-point.

"Well...." I looked down at the notebook in my lap. Last night, my mother had taken me to Drug Fair to pick out a notebook. "I can't buy a notebook until I've been to school!" I protested. "How do I know what notebook everybody will be using?" My mother thought this was the dumbest thing she had ever heard of and forced me to buy *some* kind of binder. I chose a plain blue binder, figuring that was the least offensive style of notebook until I had scoped out what everybody else was carrying. Mothers just don't understand how important the *right* things are.

"I know," I said suddenly. "We'll keep a list of the right things."

"What right things?"

"Like jewelry and clothes and hairstyles and stuff. Notebooks, even. Styles change every year, you know. We've scoured *Seven-*

teen since June, but we still could have missed something."

Gretchen looked even more nervous. "You mean, we could be wearing the wrong eye shadow?"

She could be wearing the wrong eye shadow. My makeup was limited to lip gloss and the purloined eyebrow pencil. "That's right," I told her. "One little mistake and we could end up in friendship Siberia. Remember how it was at Frost?" One of my biggest shocks in junior high was finding out the hard way that kids judge each other by the clothes they wear and the right name brands. Since then I've learned not to fight it. If you want to be in the in crowd, you have to look the part.

I opened my notebook and turned to the first clean sheet. Across the top, in jiggly handwriting, I wrote: "Right Things To Have, Get, Etc." Under that I added a series of columns headed "Makeup," "Clothes," "Hair," "Records," and "Miscellaneous." I tore out the page and gave it to Gretchen, then duplicated the list so I would have one, too.

"We'll call each other every night and report on what's new," I said.

Gretchen nodded happily. "And then we can get together on weekends and go shopping. We'll go to the mall and try things on."

13

I wasn't so sure about that. Compiling a list was one thing, but convincing my mother I *needed* all those things would be quite another. Gretchen's mother let her buy anything she wanted, but my mother was the type to make me wear the same ugly gymsuit until I was forty, simply because it still fit.

"Let's start with the list," I said. "And take it from there. One good thing about this year is that we can use these new friends we make as a sort of training ground for next year. And if things don't work out, we won't have to worry about coming back to the same school again."

This year was going to be strange for both of us. Not only was Gretchen repeating the eighth grade at Frost, but I was supposed to attend W.T. Woodson as a freshman. In August, my parents had received a copy of my class schedule along with a letter stating that four brand-new high schools were in the process of being built, and that I would attend one of those in tenth grade. In the meantime, the letter went on, I would go to Woodson, and expect it to be a little overcrowded.

Despite what I told Gretchen, I desperately wanted things to work out at Woodson. Overcrowded, temporary, I didn't care — I just wanted my freshman year to be memorable. I wanted to leave my mark.

The bus stopped and the kids standing in the aisle lurched forward.

"We're here," Gretchen said. "Get ready." Robert Frost was located just behind Woodson, so the high school kids were let off first.

I craned my neck to see out the window. "I don't see any school. Did they move it or something?"

"Better hurry," Gretchen urged. "You don't want to be late on your first day." She gave my arm a quick squeeze. "Call me tonight."

"I will. Say hi to my old art teacher if you see her." I jumped up too fast and banged my head on the overhang. A thousand anxieties attacked me: my zit, my hair, leaving Gretchen, my outfit — was it *really* okay? — starting high school!

When I stepped off the bus, I realized why I hadn't seen the school building. Our bus was at the end of a train of buses, all unloading at once.

More kids than I had ever seen in my entire life were streaming into the opened doors of Woodson. I had quite a hike before I would even reach the front door, so I hitched up my notebook and hurried across the lawn, fervently wishing I hadn't worn vinyl boots that were a size too small.

Chapter 2

To say that Woodson was a little over-crowded was like saying Yellowstone National Park had a few trees. I knew that Woodson was a big school, but there had yet to be a school built to hold all *these* kids.

Once I got inside the front door, I was immediately jammed up against the wall. I couldn't see anything, except the backs of other people. Gripping my notebook between my teeth, I managed to pull out the copy of my class schedule. My homeroom was in room Q12, wherever that was. And even if I knew where it was, I was beginning to doubt I'd get there anytime before Wednesday of the next week.

A brief break in the mob allowed me to see that floor plans of the school had been posted on the opposite wall. Now all I had to do was get over there. Contrary to popular belief, small people do not zip around in crowds, darting in and out among big people like a mouse in a furniture store. I am a small person — at age fourteen my height seemed locked at five feet three and I only weighed ninety-five pounds and that was with my shoes on and leaning a bit on the scales. What happens is that instead of zipping, I get elbowed and pushed and shoved, and the worst part of it is that people never even realize I'm *there*.

Since I couldn't zip across the lobby, I sort of allowed myself to be squashed and flattened and scuffed along like an old paper cup, until I reached the wall with the floor plans. Q12, I learned, appeared to be a little hut *outside* the actual school building. Wonderful. I could tell that being a freshman in this school was going to be one great honor after another.

"Excuse me," I said futilely to a passing senior. Seniors strode through the crowd as if they owned the place. This guy didn't even turn at the sound of my voice.

"Can you tell me — " I asked a boy wearing a varsity sweater. The boy glanced down at me with annoyance, as if I were a gnat. I thought he might even swat me.

Gamely I set off in the direction the bulk of the mob seemed to be heading. Someone stomped on my foot, already pinched in the too-tight boots. While I was limping along, two huge senior boys wedged me between them and carried me off down the hall. I felt like a tugboat berthed between the *Queen Mary* and the *Queen Elizabeth II*, but at least I didn't have to walk.

Woodson was an enormous school. There were miles of hallways, acres of lockers, hundreds of classrooms, all of which had kids hanging out the doors and windows like the old lady's shoe in the nursery rhyme. How were we all going to fit? Surely someone must have made a mistake putting this many students in one school. And where were the *teachers*? I hadn't seen a single adult since I had arrived.

Q12 was one of fifteen Quonset huts ranked like Army barracks in the back parking lot. Quonset huts were temporary structures, supposed to hold the overflow. The inside of the hut, from what little I could see, was gloomy and had the impermanent feeling of a trailer about to be driven off.

I found an empty seat and fell into it gratefully. Looking around the class, I didn't recognize anyone from Robert Frost, and certainly no one from Centreville.

The bell rang, a few more kids squeezed in, and then the door closed and I saw a real, honest-to-goodness teacher for the first time. My homeroom teacher, Mrs. Benson, apparently had been cowering behind the door. She called the roll, assigned us seats in alphabetical order, then gave out locker combinations.

The girl in front of me had short black hair and dangly plastic earrings. Her name was Cheryl Ramsey and when Mrs. Benson grouped three of us to a locker, Cheryl turned around to announce she was lockering with her boyfriend and four other guys, and to count her out.

I felt a little insulted. Had Cheryl taken one look at me and decided she didn't want to share a locker? "Won't it be rather cramped?" I asked her. Actually, I was envious — imagine sharing a locker with five boys! But since Cheryl backed out, that left me and the girl sitting behind me to share a locker. Judging from the conversations around us, the other girl and I should have been thankful. Two to a locker was a real luxury, like suddenly being accepted in a swanky country club.

I swiveled around in my seat to speak to the girl behind me.

Sandy Robertson had blonde hair and green eyes — really green, not muddied with brown or gray. When I told her that it was just the two of us in our locker, she grinned at me cheerfully.

"Hi, I'm Sandy. And you're Kobie. What a neat name. I love your outfit. Is it new? What school did you go to last year?"

"Frost," I replied, somewhat over-whelmed. Sandy certainly was friendly. But there was something about her eager, crooked grin, something about those spar-kling green eyes that set off a warning twinge inside me. Where had I seen that expression before?

"I went to Lanier," she said, oblivious of the fact that Mrs. Benson was talking. "It was a dumb school. I hear Frost is much nicer. I'm glad we're sharing a locker. I wonder if we have any other classes to-gether. Let me see your schedule."

Mrs. Benson was going on with home-room business, dull but still important. I couldn't hear a thing with Sandy yammer-ing in my ear, so I passed back my crumpled schedule to shut her up.

"Oh, great! We've got second-period home ec and last period gym together. Isn't that neat? Listen, I'll wait for you at our locker after first period, so we can go to home ec together. Okay? Okay, Kobie?"

That nattering little voice was making me dizzy. "Yeah, okay," I said, wondering if there was a class called Homeroom Part II, since I had missed everything that had gone on in mine.

The bell jangled and the class surged to-ward the door. When I stood up, I noticed a big grocery bag next to Sandy's desk. "What's that? Your lunch?"

"No, my shoes," Sandy replied, picking up the bag. It looked heavy.

"You're *wearing* your shoes." I pointed to her beat-up loafers.

"These are my *other* shoes," Sandy said, as if that explained things. "We have time to find our locker before you go to English. If we're lucky, our locker might be near your class, room 223."

I was amazed. Already Sandy had committed my schedule to memory. *I* didn't even remember I had English first period.

"What have you got first?" I asked as we flew from the parking lot into the school. Woodson's bells were timed so that we would have to sprint to every single class.

"Math," Sandy said vaguely.

"Algebra. I have it after lunch."

"Not algebra," Sandy corrected. "Math."

"Oh, maaath!" I repeated, at last catching on. Sandy was taking "dummy math," for kids not ready for algebra. To be honest, I wasn't ready for algebra myself, and would have been perfectly happy skipping the whole subject altogether, or taking a class where the most difficult assignment involved adding up the bunnies and subtracting the duckies.

There was no reason for me to act superior around Sandy, as I had signed up for "dummy algebra," a special class that split Algebra I into two years for wooden-headed students like me who needed to have equations diluted over a long period of time. Yet I felt that funny twinge again.

We located our locker without too much trouble and managed to get it open on the twenty-fourth try. Sandy put her grocery bag in the bottom. "I'll take the bottom bunk," she said. "You can have the top."

"Are you sure?" I asked. The top shelf was just right for books. The bottom part of the locker was practically useless, and storing books or anything there was like throwing rocks down a deep well. But if Sandy was going to be bringing half her wardrobe to school every day, maybe she needed the extra space.

My English class was as crowded as homeroom, but held in an actual classroom with walls and a stationary blackboard. Mrs. Ragsdale was young, blonde, and pretty. She wore Bass Weejun loafers and a Villager dress, all the "right" clothes. But she seemed more than a little terrified of such a large, seething mass of freshmen, and hopped around the front of the room like a cricket on a hot griddle. Also, she had one of those soft, ineffectual voices that didn't carry beyond the first row. Naturally I sat in the back and was going to have to learn to lip-read. I spent the period dreading our first required reading assignment, *The Merchant of Venice*, and watching Mrs. Ragsdale mouth the lecture. True to her word, Sandy Robertson met me at the door to home ec. "I think there's a free table back there," she said, leading me to the back of the room.

I gazed wistfully at the girls already settled at their tables. From their hairstyles and clothes, I knew which were the *right* girls, the ones I wanted to get in with. But those tables were filled, and I was stuck with Sandy. Maybe the teacher would shift us around and I could get at one of those other tables.

One look at Miss Channing and I realized that any hope of her doing something as complicated as rearranging the class was a lost cause. *Miss* Channing — none of that Ms. stuff for her — had to be the world's oldest living woman. She was small, with crinkly gray hair and a mouth that twisted with every syllable.

"Now, giiirls," she said, trying to get our attention.

" 'Now, giiirls,' " Sandy mimicked, twisting her mouth just like Miss Channing's. I couldn't help it, I sputtered with laughter.

Through some trick of modern medicine, Miss Channing could actually move like a greased lizard on her crepe-soled shoes. She materialized beside me like the ghost of Hamlet's father and rapped a steel-edged ruler on our table.

"What, may I ask, is so funny?" she demanded. Her eyes were flinty. "What's so funny?" she repeated.

"N-nothing," I stuttered.

"You laugh over nothing?" Miss Channing was like a bulldog with a bone. She wasn't going to let it go.

"Yeah," I replied shakily. "I do that sometimes. It's a habit — I can't control it." What could I say? That I was laughing at *her*?

"Well, you'd better control it in *my* class, young lady." Miss Channing returned to her place at the front of the room.

Sandy leaned close to me. "Whew! That was close! What a grouch she is, yelling at you like that."

I stared at her. It was *her* fault I got in trouble! While I was giggling my way into Miss Channing's little black book, Sandy had been pretending to be studying a weights and measures chart on the wall. What was *with* that girl?

"... first semester will be cooking," Miss Channing was saying. "You girls will choose your own menus and cook actual meals in our kitchens. Your grade will be based on how the dish looks and tastes."

She chuckled. "And, of course, you get to eat what you prepare."

What a treat. Home ec was not one of my favorite subjects. I wanted to take art. My life's ambition was to be an animator for Walt Disney Studios someday, to make cartoons and full-length movies like *Snow White*, but art wasn't a requirement to graduate and home ec was.

There was a knock at the door. Miss Channing admitted a blonde girl who smiled shyly and handed her a note. Obviously it was a student who had gotten lost in Woodson's maze of halls. Miss Channing jotted something in her roll book, then looked around. There weren't any extra seats, except at our table. "You can sit back there, dear," she told the new girl.

The new girl was rather large. Not fat, but *big*. She could have made two of me. Her hair wasn't blonde but yellow, a poor peroxide job. Her squinty eyes scrutinized us as she sat down. She hauled an enormous pocketbook up on the table and immediately began unloading it. Lipsticks, bottles of nail polish, jars of liquid foundation soon covered our table, more cosmetics than I had seen outside a drugstore.

"So who are you guys?" the new girl asked brusquely. We told her our names. "Is that old lady the teacher? 'You can sit there, dearie,'" she imitated, even better than Sandy had.

"What's your name?" Sandy asked her.

"Jeanette Adams." She held out a pudgy hand. On the third finger she wore a man's signet ring, wrapped with grungy-looking adhesive tape to make it fit. "See that? My boyfriend gave it to me. His name is Rob. He's a Viper."

I was about to remark that that wasn't a very nice thing to call your boyfriend, when it struck me that "Viper" was probably the name of a club or something.

Sandy, never one to be shy, came right out and asked, "What's a Viper?"

"A motorcycle gang," Jeanette replied breezily. "Rob's got a Yamaha. We go everywhere on it."

Sandy and I were both gawking at Jeanette's inch-long fingernails. "Are those real?" Sandy asked.

For an answer Jeanette reached over and dug her nails into Sandy's arm, leaving five little crescent-moon marks. Sandy stared at the bloodless dents in her wrist. I decided then and there that Jeanette Adams was not the type of person I wanted to be associated with. Jeanette was trouble.

"Miss Channing is talking," I said, hoping Sandy and Jeanette would take the hint and clam up.

"Who cares?" Jeanette uncapped a bottle

of hot-pink nail polish and began applying lacquer in long sweeping strokes.

"I don't care about her, but I need to hear what's going on," I said.

Jeanette gave me a level look. Her eyes were almost colorless, like water. "I bet you get good grades, don't you?" Her tone was contemptuous, as if making good grades was something to be ashamed of.

"I do okay," I returned.

"Kobie's real smart," Sandy put in. I don't know where she got that idea, considering we'd only met two hours before. "Does your mother let you wear all that makeup?"

Jeanette leisurely finished polishing the nails on her left hand. "My mother lets me do anything I want. She's always borrowing my stuff. We even wear each other's clothes." I couldn't imagine *wanting* to wear my mother's clothes, even if we were the same size.

"You know," Jeanette said to me, "you could use some makeup yourself."

I was only too aware that I needed major renovations, but it rankled me to have Jeanette point out my shortcomings. I wasn't irritated enough to voice my opinion, however. Jeanette scared me, though I couldn't explain why.

"How come you wear so much eye shadow?" Sandy asked. I stared at her, wondering if Sandy was really that stupid. Did she want to go through life with crescent-moon marks on her face? Jeanette Adams was not someone you willingly crossed unless you had a death wish. It occurred to me then that Sandy Robertson was not too bright and it had nothing to do with her taking dummy math. Sandy was one of those people who had the knack of always saying the wrong thing. *Open mouth, insert foot* should have been Sandy's motto.

Miss Channing was dividing the class into groups of four. Here was my chance to get away from Tweedledum and Tweedledee and into the *right* group. But when Miss Channing reached our table she said, "Well, there's just the three of you left. You'll have to be the odd table." She could say *that* again.

World geography was next. The class was held in the hall. Woodson had several short hallways that led to the center courtyard, and these had been set up as classrooms. With all these temporary arrangements, I was beginning to feel like the man without a country. Mr. Eaton was young and good-looking, and he liked to kid around. I could use a laugh. So far this day had been anything but funny.

I noticed two girls in the front row. Marianne Andrews had long taffy-colored hair and a slow, pretty smile that revealed great teeth. She talked with a slight drawl, and at once I decided I wanted to be like Marianne, cool and pretty, not frenzied and sweaty. Behind her sat Barbara Phillips, who was so skinny she looked like something assembled out of wire scraps, but she wore an expensive matching skirt and blouse and a gold circle pin on her collar. Marianne and Barbara were obviously friends and talked all through Mr. Eaton's terrible jokes. Those two had that elusive quality I was looking for — they were definitely the *right* people.

After geography was lunch, which might have been nice if I had found the cafeteria in time to eat. Then came algebra, another class in the hall, and then French, in a Quonset hut. My French teacher was tall and beautiful and let us know within twelve seconds of the bell that she was once Miss Arizona. The boys looked very eager for French lessons.

My last class of the day was phys ed. By a stroke of luck, I managed to have it at the best possible time. Gym first period meant you had to go through the rest of the day looking like an earthquake victim, because you could never get yourself pulled together right after being mauled around on the volleyball court. Gym right before or after lunch was not good for the digestive system. Gym at the end of the day was perfect. Nobody cared how you looked getting on the bus to go home.

I recognized some girls from my other classes. Marianne Andrews and her friend Barbara Phillips. Cheryl Ramsey from homeroom. And Sandy Robertson, who spotted me at once and came galloping over. I had totally forgotten that Sandy was going to be in my gym class.

"I missed you at lunch," Sandy said, as if we'd been separated for twenty years. "What shift do you have?"

"I don't know. I never got to the cafeteria."

"Maybe I can get my lunch shift changed to yours. Wouldn't that be great?"

"Peachy." I was tired. My feet, stuffed into those too-small boots, were sending me signals. One more step, they warned, and we quit, go on strike, walk off the job.

Ms. Birmingham blew a whistle and had us all sit on the floor. I was getting used to the first-class accommodations Woodson offered freshmen. The teacher called the roll, and as she did, assigned us gym locker partners. Guess who mine was. Sandy Robertson.

"Look, there's Jeanette," Sandy said.

Sure enough, the Avon lady was late again. She handed Ms. Birmingham her note, now ragged around the edges. Ms. Birmingham introduced her to the class as *Peggy* Adams.

"Peggy?" Sandy piped up. "I thought your name was Jeanette! That's what you said in home ec."

Ms. Birmingham looked questioningly at Peggy/Jeanette. "Well, which is it? Peggy or Jeanette?"

"Both, but I'd rather go by Peggy in here," Jeanette said. I wondered if Jeanette had a whole purseful of aliases, along with written excuses to teachers and all her makeup.

Jeanette gave Sandy a withering glance as she sat down beside us.

"Sorry," Sandy whispered. "I didn't mean to make a big deal."

"It's okay," Peggy/Jeanette said, but her tone implied just the opposite. She didn't speak to me, but once again I sensed trouble with that girl. And I fully intended to stay out of her way.

I looked over at Sandy. She seemed like a nice girl, but there was *something* about her. Her dress was a notch above the Ugliest Dress in the World, the hand-me-down I was forced to wear on the first day of school last year. But it wasn't just her clothes. Sandy had the too-desperate expression of a loser. She could never get into the *right* crowd, even if she sported Villager labels from head to toe. And neither could I, if I didn't ditch her.

The minute I got home I called Gretchen.

"I've been waiting forever," she said. "Kobie, I've had such a horrible day!"

"You!" I bellowed into the receiver. "Gretchen, my day was the absolute *pits*! You won't *believe* the stuff that happened to me." And I proceeded to tell her about Sandy and Jeanette.

"I want to get in with the right crowd," I complained. "Instead, I wind up saddled with those two! I'm probably already marked. Nobody popular will want to touch me with a ten-foot pole! I have to get rid of them!"

Gretchen sympathized with me. "This Sandy sounds like she's going to be tough to get rid of. I think you've met your match, Kobie."

Maybe. But I felt more as if I had met my Waterloo.

Chapter 3

"I'm writing my Congressman," I announced, "to tell him the first day of school ought to be followed by a week of holidays."

"Make it a year of holidays, and I'll sign it, too," Gretchen said.

We were in my bedroom. It was Friday evening and Gretchen had come over to have supper with me.

"Do you have corned beef hash and peas with cream soda *every* Friday?" Gretchen asked.

Lately my parents had started eating around ten on Friday evenings. Since I ate by myself at a reasonable hour, my mother fixed whatever I wanted. After a few false starts with TV dinners, I fell into a corned-beef-hash-Green-Giant-peas groove and could look forward to those delicacies on Friday nights.

"Every Friday," I said. "At first Mom

tried to tempt me with stuff like cubed steak and instant mashed potatoes, but I said no dice. Peas and hash or nothing. Look, here's that sock. I thought I'd lost it." I pulled out my missing kneesock from beneath the covers.

I hadn't made my bed since school started, despite my mother's incessant harping. "Why bother?" I'd argue. "I just have to mess it up again at night."

"That's no excuse," my mother would say. "You're a slob, Kobie Roberts."

"Well, everybody has to be something."

"It's not funny. If you don't learn to do these things now, when will you? I pity the poor man who marries you." And on and on, until I'd finally throw the covers up over my socks and pajamas to pacify her.

Now I asked Gretchen, "Is your mother impossible these days?"

"Yes. She's always yelling at me to turn down my record player."

"I don't know what I'm going to do with mine," I said. "She was off my case while she was learning to drive, but now she's back to her old grouchy self."

At the age of forty-eight, my mother decided she was tired of depending on other people for rides to the store and she wanted to get her license. She and Dad spent most of last summer in the big empty lot behind the county jail, parallel parking and undoubtedly entertaining the inmates.

"Forget mothers," Gretchen said. "Are we going over our lists or not?"

I slid off my bed and dug out my notebook from beneath a pile of drawing books. "I barely had time to notice anything last week," I said. "Woodson is such a zoo. I don't know how I'm going to survive a whole year there."

Gretchen pulled her list from her purse. "Be thankful you aren't going to be in the same school all your life. The same *grade* all your life. Did I tell you I have the same teachers for English, earth science, and gym as I did last year?"

"Well, look at it this way — at least you don't have to break them in."

She pulled at a tuft of bedspread in despair. "I hate repeating a grade. And what's worse is I'll miss my freshman year if I go to summer school. I feel cheated."

"Believe me, you aren't missing a thing. Being a freshman has nothing whatsoever to recommend it. Upperclassmen treat us like insects."

Gretchen didn't seem convinced. Unable to think of anything else to say, I picked up my list.

"Here are the right things kids are wearing at Woodson. Weejuns and Villagers, natch. Circle pins. Geometric haircuts. And pierced ears. Most of the girls wear earrings that dangle."

Gretchen nodded. "Girls at Frost wear those, too." She consulted her list. "Weejuns and Villagers, sweaters, skirts and kneesocks that match. Circle pins. Oh, and Ambush cologne. All the girls wear Ambush. The boys wear English Leather."

"How do you get close enough to boys to smell their cologne?" I asked, suspicious. Did Gretchen have a boyfriend already, the first week of school?

"You don't have to get close," she replied tartly. "They shower with the stuff."

I added Ambush to my own list. "What are you going to get first? The sooner we start getting the right things, the sooner we can get into the right crowd."

Gretchen checked off an item on her list and showed it to me. "This."

"You're going to get your ears pierced?" I said in awe. "Your mother will let you?"

Gretchen nodded. "I think so. I already asked her, and she didn't fall down and tear her hair out like I thought she would."

I was envious. "Your mother must not be as far-gone as you think." But mine was, I knew. "The only way I'll ever get my ears pierced is if one of the planes flying into Dulles Airport breaks the sound barrier."

Gretchen giggled. "That would pierce your ear*drums*, stupid."

"Whatever. In this world you have to take what you can get." Dulles International Airport was only a few miles from our house. The jets flew over very low and ruined what little television reception we had. "When are you getting it done?"

"Maybe next weekend. Want to come with me?"

I thought it over and decided I didn't really want to watch Gretchen getting holes punched in her earlobes. If by chance my mother became delirious and let me get my ears pierced, I'd only have it done under general anesthetic.

"What are *you* going to get first?" Gretchen said, still on the subject of our lists.

I fell back on my pillows, discouraged. "Nothing. It wouldn't matter if I got my ears pierced twenty times and had Villager labels tattooed all over my body. I'll never get in the right crowd, not as long as I'm stuck with Laurel and Hardy."

"You told me you were going to ditch Sandy and — what's that girl's name?"

"She's Jeanette in home ec and Peggy in gym and trouble any way you look at it." I sat up. "Gretchen, you have no idea what she's like. Jeanette never dresses for gym. She's got a fake doctor's excuse that says she's too frail to take gym. Frail! She's built like a tank! And she scares me to death."

"How?" Gretchen asked.

"I don't know exactly. She's never done anything to me specifically, but I think she has it in for me." I took a few seconds to organize my thoughts. "Jeanette is one of those people who never does what she's supposed to and gets away with it. You know how some people break all the rules but never get paid back? Jeanette's like that — untouchable and . . . dangerous. She even has a boyfriend who's a Viper. That's a motorcycle gang."

Gretchen's eyebrows shot up. "She goes with a guy who's in a motorcycle gang? In ninth grade?"

"I think she's older than she's supposed to be. I bet she's been left back."

"Well, I know how *that* feels," Gretchen said wryly.

"Gretch, you've got a perfectly good reason for being left back — you were in an accident. Peggy probably flunked because she doesn't *do* anything in class except put on her makeup."

"And the teacher lets her get away with it?"

I snorted. "You don't know Miss Channing. The woman is definitely not wrapped too tight. It's the weirdest thing — Peggy sits back there and runs her yap the whole period, not in a whisper, either, and Miss Channing never hears a thing. If I open my mouth to breathe, she's on me like a duck on a June bug."

"Maybe this Jeanette has something on the old woman," Gretchen suggested.

"She'd be the type to blackmail," I agreed. "The thing is, between her and Sandy, I'm going crazy. Not to mention I haven't the faintest idea what's going on in home ec. Monday we have to cook our first meal, and I don't have a single note written down."

"You'll fake it," Gretchen assured me. "But what about that Sandy? She's the one I'd worry about, if I were you. She sounds really strange. You told me you were going to dump her."

I stared at my list of right things. "I was."

"What happened?"

"It was her shoes," I replied. "Her shoes did me in. See, Sandy brings this great big grocery bag to school every day and puts it in our locker. When I asked her what it was, she said it was her shoes, but I can see she's got shoes on her feet. So finally I opened the bag one day when she wasn't around."

Gretchen leaned forward. "And what was in it?"

"Shoes. Ugly, clunky shoes. One of them had an extra-thick heel, about two inches high. I asked Sandy about them and she said they were orthopedic shoes. She had polio when she was little and one leg is shorter than the other. She's supposed to wear these shoes, but they're so ugly, she can't stand to be seen in them. She wears the corrective shoes on the bus and changes into regular shoes at school, so her mother won't find out. She does limp when she walks. And that's why I haven't dumped her."

Gretchen smiled. "You're just an old softie, Kobie Roberts."

"Just an old dumbbell, you mean."

Monday in second period, I found out just how dumb I really was.

Our table was the last to make lunch. Jeanette went over to the dinette table at the other end of the test kitchen and plopped herself down.

"What are you doing sitting down?" I asked her. "We've got to cook lunch."

"Not me." Jeanette emptied the contents of her purse, just as she did every day in home ec. "I'm not fooling around with a bunch of old pots and pans."

I couldn't believe she was refusing to take part in the project. "You *have* to. It's part of our grade."

Jeanette gave me one of her penetrating stares. "Read my lips. I'm not doing any work. But you are, so you'd better get busy."

Sandy tugged at my arm. "Forget her, Kobie. She's not going to help and that's that."

I walked over to the table, aware that behind me was a rack filled with sharp knives and meat cleavers. If Jeanette wanted to get nasty, there were plenty of weapons at her disposal.

"Let me get this straight," I said to her. "Sandy and I are going to knock ourselves out on all the cooking projects and you aren't going to lift a finger."

Jeanette propped her hand mirror against a soup tureen. "You catch on fast. *But*," she added warningly, "I expect you guys to do a good job. This is my grade, too, you know."

There wasn't anything I could do. Trying to get Jeanette to cooperate would be like asking a stone wall to move. And tattling to Miss Channing was worse than useless — she acted like Jeanette was made out of cake.

"What are we fixing?" I asked Sandy.

"Jeanette put us down for tomato soup and toasted cheese sandwiches," Sandy replied.

"*Jeanette* picked out what we're going to cook, knowing she wasn't even going to help?" I glared back at Jeanette who was busy curling her eyelashes.

"Kobie, we haven't much time," Sandy said.

"All right. I'll make the soup and you do the sandwiches." Raising my voice a degree, I said, "I don't suppose Jeanette would like to set the table?"

"You suppose right," came the answer. "Did I ever tell you girls about the bikers' picnic Rob took me to last summer?"

I rummaged through the cupboards. "Sandy, where's the soup? Miss Channing said she bought the groceries we'd need, but I don't see any soup."

"Are you listening to me?" Jeanette demanded. I nodded, even though I hadn't heard a word of her dumb story.

"We have to make it from scratch," Sandy said, getting a hunk of cheese out of the refrigerator.

"Tomato soup from scratch!" I shrieked. "Nobody makes tomato soup from scratch! You open up a can and add water!" I forced myself to calm down. Hysteria would not get the soup made. "Sandy, what goes in tomato soup?"

Sandy hacked off a slice of cheese, which fell on the floor. Dusting it off, she said thoughtfully, "Tomatoes — "

"*That* much I figured." I slammed a can of whole tomatoes on the counter. "What else?"

"I don't know. I've never heard of anybody making tomato soup either. It's always *there*. Kobie, do you think I should slice the cheese in little pieces or try to make big slices like you get in the store?"

"This is ridiculous. How are we supposed to cook without recipes?" The other girls took their notebooks into the kitchens and referred to their class notes. But because I sat between two blabbermouths, I had no notes, no recipes, no idea what I was doing.

"Better hurry, girls," Jeanette sang out. "You have to have lunch on the table by quarter of eleven."

It was ten-thirty. "You can't cook soup in fifteen minutes," I said. "Sandy, quick, tell me what goes *in* this stuff!"

Sandy was at the other counter, mutilating slices of bread as she buttered them. "Tomatoes — "

"We *said* that already! I can't serve a bowl of tomatoes! Tomato soup is *liquid*!"

And then I got the bright idea of draining the water the tomatoes were packed in into the pan. The liquid looked pinkish and anemic and very unsouplike. Then I remembered seeing my mother add milk and butter in her soup.

Twenty-five of eleven. I poured in milk and turned the burner under the pan as high as it would go.

"Do these look okay?" Sandy held out a plate containing three pitiful cheese sandwiches. The bread was cratered from her ruthless buttering.

My soup was boiling furiously. I dumped in a big glob of butter and ran to set the table, which wasn't easy, as I had to work around Jeanette's beauty parlor.

I ran back to check my soup. Instead of the thick creamy liquid I expected, I saw to my horror that the milk had formed cottage cheese lumps and that something, probably the butter, had turned brown. "We can't eat this! We'll just have to tell Miss Channing the soup didn't turn out. How are those sandwiches coming, Sandy?"

"I think they're stuck. I can't get them out of the toaster."

"Toaster! You're supposed to cook them in a skillet!"

"How was I to know?"

Sandy had put our cheese sandwiches,

buttered side out, in the toaster! The cheese had melted, glomming up the works. I unplugged the toaster and dug out the sandwiches with a knife. Arranged on a platter, the blistered cheese sandwiches looked only slightly better than my soup with its blobs of curdled milk floating like marshmallows on the surface of brownish-pink scum.

"Can't you guys do anything right?" Jeanette said in disgust. "That stuff's not fit for dogs."

"Ahhh! Something smells — *interesting*," Miss Channing remarked, coming in with the rest of the class. The kitchen smelled like charred cheese and scorched milk, hardly aromas to whet an appetite.

Cautiously, Miss Channing removed the lid from the soup tureen and the cover from the sandwich platter. "Oh!" She stepped back at the sight of our pathetic lunch. The other girls snickered. "Well, I'm supposed to sample your cooking," Miss Channing stalled, "but I'm afraid I can't. I've got a cold sore." She was chicken. "Enjoy your lunch, girls. Don't forget to clean up before you leave."

She and the rest of the class went back to the home ec room, leaving the three of us to eat that dreadful soup.

"I'm not touching that slop," Jeanette stated.

"We *have* to eat it," Sandy said. "Miss Channing will know if we don't." The dinette table was in full view of the home ec room, separated only by a counter.

"*You* eat it. I'm getting something decent to eat." Jeanette got up and searched through the cupboards, coming back with a box of Ritz crackers and a can of something she called "pat-tay."

Sandy's sandwiches had all the appeal of burned rubber, but my soup was positively revolting. I shuddered with every spoonful. We had to gobble down our share plus Jeanette's before cleaning up that hogpen kitchen.

Jeanette spread a grayish-looking substance on a cracker. Of course, Miss Channing never noticed what she was eating. I was surprised the teacher didn't serve her pheasant under glass.

"What is that stuff?" I asked.

"Haven't you ever had pâté?" She fixed me a cracker and handed it to me, her face bland and deceptively innocent.

I sniffed at it, then decided it couldn't be any worse than my own cooking. I ate the cracker in two bites before I realized that it tasted funny, like the time I ate a fried oyster. "What did I just eat?"

Jeanette smiled wickedly. "Goose livers. Mashed goose livers."

Chapter 4

Every day in world geography, Marianne Andrews sat sideways in her chair so she could talk to Barbara Phillips, who sat behind her, and snipped her split ends with manicure scissors. Amazingly, Mr. Eaton paid no attention to her except to remark once that by Christmas her hair would probably be as short as his. I watched Marianne from my desk two rows over as she ran her fingers through long silky strands, selected an offending split end, and flashed those silver scissors. Snip, snip. It was mesmerizing.

And every day in geography, the boy who sat across the aisle from me watched *me*. His name was Eddie Showalter. He was a stocky boy about my height, with dark hair and dark eyes, and thick wiggly eyebrows like caterpillars. He wore the same beige cardigan sweater no matter what the weather was.

While I gaped at Marianne Andrews, longing to be casually indifferent like her, Eddie Showalter watched me out of the corner of his eye. Instead of taking notes in class, he doodled in the margins of his textbook and the ditto sheets Mr. Eaton passed around. Always interested in a fellow artist, I peeked at Eddie's drawings one day when he got up to sharpen his pencil. There were sketches of the White House — *the* White House, as in the President's residence — and finely detailed drawings of jet airplanes. That was it. The White House and jets. I dismissed Eddie Showalter as a Class A weirdo and wished he would stop staring at me.

On the day of the bungled home ec lunch, I was late for geography, owing to acute indigestion from forcing down that ghastly soup and having to clean up the kitchen, which resembled a disaster site. Mr. Eaton didn't say anything — he even let me in without a pass. Miss Channing had flat out refused to write Sandy and me a pass. She had drilled us with her gimlet eyes and lectured us on the importance of not fooling around in class, so I had only a mumbled excuse to offer Mr. Eaton.

I sat down and opened my geography book, but visions of curdled soup and goose liver crackers passed before my eyes in a pinkish tomato-soup-colored haze. I burped discreetly behind my hand and wondered how anyone had the gall to mash up goose livers and sell it as a food.

I felt a note slipped under my elbow. From Marianne Andrews, maybe wanting to be friends? I unfolded the paper to reveal a curly-haired stick figure, presumably me, hanging out of the open cockpit of an old-fashioned airplane. At least he had my measurements right — definitely not from Marianne. The caption read, "Are you sick?"

I looked up. Eddie Showalter was doodling aimlessly in his geography book and for once not watching me. But I could tell by the tense way he gripped his pencil that he had sent the note and he knew I knew he'd sent it.

Yes, I scribbled on the bottom of the cartoon, sick of school.

I tossed the folded note on his desk, so he would catch on that I didn't really want this conversation to continue. He read it, smiled faintly, then went back to his doodling.

Later on that week, I saw Eddie during lunch. I had finally discovered the location of the cafeteria, a huge facility with two separate kitchens and serving lines. The eating area was partitioned down the center with a metal divider. There were four lunch periods, the first starting at an improbable ten-thirty, and each period was divided into two groups, making a total of eight lunch shifts. I had been assigned the very last time slot, and ate in "B" cafeteria.

The good tables were taken by upperclassmen, leaving the dregs near the garbage cans for the hapless freshmen. Even then I had trouble finding a seat. The serving lines were always long, and I always got to the cafeteria late, so I often found myself wandering around with my tray, hunting for an empty seat like a rescue boat searching for the survivors of a shipwreck. Once I simply propped my tray on top of a garbage can lid and ate standing up. Given the quality of high school cuisine, there wasn't much difference between the food on my plate and the stuff dumped in the trash.

I saw Eddie Showalter about the same time he spotted me. He was sitting at the end of a table. There was an empty seat across from him. He motioned for me to join him, wiggling his funny eyebrows and grinning as if it would be the greatest thing in the world if I sat with him. How bad could it be? The worst he could do would be to draw the White House on my paper napkin. I was heading for Eddie's table when a voice cut through the lunchtime racket.

"Kobie Roberts! Over here!" Stuart Buckley was standing on a chair and waving like mad.

I gave Eddie an apologetic what-can-I-do-I'm-so-popular smile and went over to Stuart's table instead.

Stuart Buckley had been my nemesis in eighth grade. His locker had been next to mine and he had driven me crazy the whole year by slamming it shut and generally endearing himself to me by knocking over my chair one day at lunch (while I was still in it) and blowing up my cat statue in art class. But as the year progressed and I became immune to Stuart's pranks, I also got to know him better. He was very short and apparently had a Napoleon complex, which explained his awful behavior, most of the time. Stuart had troubles at home — his father had remarried and his new stepmother didn't want him around. When school ended last year, Stuart's grandmother was trying to get custody of him.

"Kobie!" Stuart cried. "Where have you *been* all year?"

I plunked down my tray and began frantically eating my lunch. I had four minutes until my next class. "Right here, Stuart. Along with the other nine thousand kids in this school. What's happening with you? Are you staying with your grandmother now?"

Stuart helped himself to my dessert, just like old times. "Yeah. It's really great. She lets me do anything I want. Some nights I don't go to bed till one or two."

Last year Stuart had had to wait outside his own house until his stepmother came home from work and let him in. Now he was whooping it up at his grandmother's. Leave it to Stuart to go from one extreme to the other.

"How do you like Woodson?" I asked him.

"It's okay. Listen, Kobie, do you have a dollar I can borrow?"

"Don't tell me you don't have lunch money again. Doesn't your grandmother give you any?"

"Yeah, but something came up today and I need an extra dollar. Can you loan me?" Stuart put on his puppy-dog expression. How could I resist?

"I only have fifty cents," I said, reaching for my purse.

Stuart took the two quarters and catapulted himself out of his chair, planting a very sloppy kiss on top of my head. "Thanks, Kobie! You're a real sport! See you around!"

And he was off. Real Sport ate the rest

of her lunch alone, wondering if she was ever going to have any friends, much less the right ones.

Riding in the car with my mother since she had gotten her driver's license was hardly the big thrill I thought it would be. I imagined my mother and I jumping in the car and cruising to Manassas to hit the shops anytime we felt like it.

In actuality, my mother metered her trips as if she were only allowed a certain number each week and planned them hours and even days in advance. She labored over every left-hand turn she'd have to make and plotted the best approaches into parking spots, so she'd be pointed in the right direction when it was time to go home again, with all the strategy of a general preparing for battle.

So when she asked me to go with her to the carpet store in Kamp Washington on Friday afternoon, I didn't exactly spring up at the opportunity. I was in a rotten mood anyway. Gretchen was getting her ears pierced that weekend and the most I had to look forward to was standing around a bunch of rugs. I wanted to be left alone, to eat my corned beef hash and canned peas and then drown my sorrows in cream soda.

"Stop pouting and come with me," my

mother persisted. "I need help picking out a color."

I got into our Chevy without argument, fastened the seat belt, and sat rigidly with my arms pasted to my sides so my mother wouldn't be distracted by any stray hand movements. She put the car into gear with only a few fumbles and we crept out of the driveway. My mother drove in white-knuckled terror down the road, her eyes switching from windshield to rearview mirror like a metronome as she scanned the surrounding highway for berserk dump trucks, and muttered that she hoped the guy in the van in front of her didn't suddenly have a heart attack. I wasn't permitted to play the radio or even to talk, except to warn her of impending calamity.

Bill's Carpet Barn was located next to People's Drug Store.

"I'm going in there," I informed her, an ulterior motive up my sleeve. "I need school supplies."

"I just bought you school supplies," my mother said, inching into a slot and checking the side mirrors to make sure she didn't total any nearby cars, even though they were practically in the next county. "What happened to all that stuff we got before school started?"

"Mom, nobody at Woodson carries a dumb old ring binder. I need spiral notebooks, one for each subject, and a cartridge pen." I loved the idea of writing with a cartridge ink pen. The ink flowed through the tip like liquid velvet and made me want to write in my best handwriting.

"Where do you keep your homework?" Mom asked. "And notebook paper? I know your teachers don't like paper ripped out of spiral notebooks."

"In my books," I replied.

"You fold up paper instead of keeping it nice in a perfectly good binder?"

"Mo-om! You want me to look like a first-grader? Why don't you make me carry a bookbag and a Snoopy lunchbox? Can I go in People's and get the stuff or not?"

"We'll see," my mother said. "Come with me to pick out carpeting first."

I don't know why my mother asked for my opinion on what color wall-to-wall carpeting to get for our living room. She made a beeline straight to the color she wanted, a dull olive green, and the salesman began writing up her order.

I sat on a clump of carpet swatches, mad at the world. My mother would probably agree to new school supplies if I wore her down, but she sure wasn't going to let me get a bottle of Ambush cologne, the real reason I wanted to go to People's. She wasn't going to let me do anything, not ever. I might as well throw away my list of right things for all the good it was doing me.

I was still seething over Gretchen getting her ears pierced when I heard the salesman say, "Will there be anything else?"

"Yes!" I blurted out before my mother could speak. "I need a rug for my bedroom. Isn't that right, Mom?"

"Kobie, you know we only came for living room carpeting today," she said evenly.

The salesman rubbed his hands together. "We have some wonderful buys in room-size remnants."

"Let's go look at them," I said.

"Kobie — "

"Aw, Mom! You're fixing up the living room, why not my room, too? I've never had a carpet, and my room is the coldest in the Northern Hemisphere." That much was true. My room faced the northwest corner and got all the freezing winds. In the winter I slept with so many quilts on my bed that my toes were permanently curled under from the weight.

"Don't start, Kobie," my mother warned.

"Who's starting anything? All I'm asking for is a rug on my cold, bare floor."

"You *have* a rug!"

"Only a little skimpy one, and it's real old. Come on, Mom," I wheedled. I was a good wheedler. Last year I whined myself into all sorts of new things. I was amazed the same tactic still worked.

The salesman was clearly on my side. He looked as if he wanted to say to my mother, "Give the kid a break, you big bully!" but he kept his composure as he led us over to the remnant section.

My mother sighed. "I suppose it's time you got something for your room. But you have to promise me, Kobie, that you'll keep your room clean and I mean *clean* if I get you a carpet."

"Yeah, sure. Hey, Mom, how about this one?" I pointed to a royal purple rug, so bright it should have come supplied with a glare screen.

My mother wrinkled her nose. "No, that won't do at all. Here's a nice one." She indicated a brown tweedy carpet. "This is a sensible weave and brown will go with your furniture."

"I hate brown!" I said vehemently. "Brown, brown, brown! Everything I own is brown! I've had nothing but brown dresses my whole life, like a poor kid!"

"You're going to be a poor *dead* kid if you don't cut it out," my mother said in an undertone.

"I don't want brown!" I yelled. The salesman looked alarmed, as if he were on the verge of calling the men in the white coats. "I want the purple rug! If you really loved me you wouldn't make me sleep in a brown room. You'd buy me that purple rug and get me turquoise curtains and a lime-green bedspread!"

"Kobie, what's the matter with you?" She snatched me by the arm, not caring if the salesman was watching. "Purple and turquoise in a bedroom! Where do you get such notions?"

"I've always wanted a purple and turquoise and lime-green color scheme," I said. "Those are my very favorite colors. If you wouldn't keep me strapped in brown, you'd know that."

"Don't get smart with me, young lady," my mother said, but it seemed a little late for that. I had already gotten smart with her and in front of a salesman, too.

I couldn't keep it up. Last year I had pitched some terrific fits to get what I wanted, but now I felt old and defeated. What difference did it make if I slept in an ugly brown room or a beautiful purple one? I was still Kobie Roberts, with stupid hair and no figure and intact earlobes. Tears sprang into my eyes. My mother saw them and must have thought I was crying because I wanted the purple carpet so badly.

"We'll take the purple one," she told the salesman wearily. "It's what she wants."

I walked over to the window and looked

out. Why had I wasted a perfectly good tantrum on a dumb old rug? I should have waited until we went into People's and pleaded for Ambush cologne. No way I'd ever get it now.

Chapter 5

I didn't talk to Gretchen over the weekend. She called me on both Saturday and Sunday, but both times I let my mother answer the phone and told her to tell Gretchen I was busy. Well, one of those times I *was* in the bathtub, nervously shaving my legs with my father's razor. But I could have called Gretchen right back. I didn't because I didn't want to hear about her pierced ears. All I had gotten out of the weekend was a purple rug.

By Monday I was feeling pretty crummy. Why shouldn't Gretchen crow about her pierced ears? No wonder I didn't have any friends — I wasn't very nice to the one friend I had. So when I got on the bus and found Gretchen huddled in a corner of the backseat, I told her I was sick the whole weekend and made a big fuss over the little gold studs in her ears.

Gretchen eagerly rotated the posts in her earlobes. "There isn't anything to it, Kobie. It hardly hurt at all. I have to turn my earrings and put alcohol on them twice a day and that's it. You should talk to your mother about it."

I stared morosely out the bus window. "I can't talk to my mother about anything, much less earrings. We bought carpeting Friday afternoon and now she's worried she spent too much money, but it's too late because the carpet people are bringing the stuff out later this week."

"Do you think you can come over this weekend?"

"I hope so. Unless the world comes to an end. I still have to survive another whole week at Woodson, you know."

The world didn't come to an end. In fact, the week was almost pleasant. Jeanette was out sick, so that left me and Sandy Robertson alone at our table in home ec. With only one of the two blabbermouths there, I could occasionally catch snatches of Miss Channing's lesson, although my head had the funny feeling you get when you play a stereo with only one speaker.

Miss Channing was supposed to be lecturing us on the art of pie-making. But she seemed a little mixed up because the whole time she was demonstrating how to roll out a pie crust, she held a plastic baby doll to her shoulder. Evidently, she had lectured the class before ours on diapering babies. The baby doll kept slipping, and once or twice it fell in the pie dough, but Miss Channing didn't seem to care. She merely picked it up, scraped dough off its face, and clasped it to her shoulder, which was draped with a tea towel, and made her look as if she were burping the doll.

"Look at her," Sandy said, during her running commentary. "That woman doesn't know which end is up. Now she's holding the doll upside-down! She'll probably forget and diaper the doll with pie dough!"

It wouldn't have surprised me either. Miss Channing was one of those chronically absentminded people. Today she wore two pairs of glasses, one pair on her face and the other perched forgotten on top of her forehead. Home ec was turning into a real trip.

Sandy grew bored joking about the teacher and idly opened my algebra textbook. "Can you do the stuff in here?"

"Barely. It's one of those classes in the hall, and I only hear about every other sentence." I hoped Sandy would take the hint.

She was examining a folded piece of notebook paper stuck between the pages. "What's this?" She angled the paper so I could see it.

My face flamed with embarrassment. My right things list! I tried to grab it away from her. "Nothing. Put it back."

Instantly Miss Channing was breathing down my neck. "What's going on over here, giiirls?" she demanded.

I decided to quit protecting Sandy, who was forever getting me in trouble with that woman. "She's got my paper. I told her to put it back, that's all."

Miss Channing glowered at me. For a second, I thought she might club me with the plastic baby doll. "Kobie, give Sandy back her paper."

"No, wait! See, it's *my* paper — I'm trying to get it back from *her*!"

"Do you hear me, Kobie? I said give Sandy back her paper, and I don't want any more disruptions from this table."

With clenched teeth and murder in my heart, I handed Sandy *my* paper. Miss Channing clucked in satisfaction, then went back to her diapering/pie-making demonstration.

"I'm sorry, Kobie," Sandy said. "I didn't know she'd hear us. Here, take your paper. I didn't read hardly any of it."

I slumped in my chair. "Forget it, Sandy. Read it if you want." I couldn't for the life of me understand why Sandy and Jeanette could talk in class at the top of their lungs and get away with it, while Miss Channing jumped down my throat if I even thought about talking. Had someone nominated me this year's poster girl for a "Life Is Unfair" campaign?

Sandy was dragging me down, no doubt about it. Because of an unimaginative school system that clumped everybody alphabetically and a fluke in our last names, we were destined to go through ninth grade linked together. If I didn't break free of Sandy, I would lose any chance of getting into Marianne Andrews' select little group, and I could look forward to another eight months of Miss Channing's wrath and inedible home ec meals.

"Wow, this is really neat," Sandy remarked. "You've made a list of all the good stuff to get. What a great idea!"

"Not so great," I said gloomily. "So far I haven't gotten one thing on that list."

"It's still a good idea." Sandy opened her own notebook and began copying my headings. "I'm making one, too. Some of the things on here aren't very expensive. Like that Ambush cologne and the makeup. I could buy those out of my allowance. We ought to go shopping together sometime. What do you say?"

I didn't trust myself to reply. Sandy was copying *my* list, the list I had made for Gretchen and myself, and now she wanted to go shopping with me. She acted as if we were best friends or something. What nerve! If I hadn't gotten all sentimental over her orthopedic shoes, I would have told Sandy off long ago. But how do you reject somebody who once had polio? Maybe I could stop by Miss Channing's desk after class and tell her I wanted my seat changed.

Sandy finished copying my list and slipped the paper back in my algebra book. "You know, Kobie, I'm so glad you sit with me. Nobody else does in my other classes. I've never really had a good friend before. I'm going to start getting the things on this list because I want to be just like you. You do everything just right."

So much for asking to have my seat changed.

Jeanette Adams was out for over a week, but when she came back to school, we all knew it. She dumped her two-ton pocketbook on our home ec table and fished around inside for a note, which she took to Miss Channing.

"You must have been real sick," Sandy said to her.

"I was, part of the time," Jeanette admitted. "The rest of the time I skipped. Remind me to fix this note."

Today it was our table's turn in the kitchen. As usual, I hadn't a clue as to what

65

was going on. "What are we making?" I asked Sandy.

She handed me an apron. "Banana cream pie. Remember, last week we had the unit on pies?"

My pie-making knowledge was scrambled up with diapering baby dolls. "Who put us down for banana cream?"

"I did," Jeanette said from her place at the dinette table. "It's my favorite kind."

"How did you tell Miss Channing what kind of pie we were making when you were out a week and a half? By proxy?"

Jeanette didn't answer, but sat hunched over the excuse her mother had written her, with a bottle of Wite-Out, preparing to alter the contents.

In no time, the kitchen was a blizzard of sifted flour. Sandy made the crust while I toiled over the custard filling and Jeanette interrupted with questions like, "How do you spell appendicitis?" and "Does tonsil have one *l* or two?" Jeanette hadn't been back to school three hours and already she was making me an accessory to forgery.

The pie was cooling on the dinette table and Jeanette was blowing on her forged excuse to dry the Wited-Out parts when Miss Channing sailed in with the class.

"It looks beautiful, girls," Miss Channing cooed. "Kobie, will you serve your creation?"

I cut the first slice and transferred it to a dessert plate. That was when I noticed the white strings mingled in with the cream filling and that the layer of bananas on the bottom had turned an unappetizing brown.

"Gross!" one girl cried. "What's that stringy stuff!"

"Cooked egg," Miss Channing diagnosed. "Somebody wasn't paying attention in class when I went over how to beat eggs properly. Somebody failed to separate her eggs and beat the yokes thoroughly." Somebody certainly had and I knew who she was. Miss Channing made another mark in her gradebook, then said, gleefully, *"Bon appétit, girls!"*

"No way," Jeanette said.

I agreed. Nobody was going to force me to eat that horrible gooey pie with those stringy egg whites and moldy-looking bananas and I said so.

Sandy said, "I'll eat Jeanette's piece, Kobie. If you close your eyes, you won't even see the egg part."

Somehow I made it through the rest of the day, until gym class. Of course Ms. Birmingham had chosen a regimen of exercises that involved a lot of stomach-unsettling jumping around for us to do that day. As Sandy and I changed into our gymsuits, we saw Jeanette give Ms. Birmingham her altered excuse.

"You know," Sandy said loudly. "I bet Jeanette forgot to change that part about the dates like she said she was going to."

Ms. Birmingham heard Sandy. Jeanette heard Sandy. Anyone not wearing lead earmuffs heard Sandy. Ms. Birmingham took another look at Jeanette's note, then told the class to begin without her, she had a little matter to attend to. She ushered Jeanette into her office. Jeanette glared at Sandy with eyes that could have dissolved reinforced steel.

After class, Sandy and I scanned the locker room for Jeanette, but saw no sign of her.

"She was furious," I said to Sandy. "She's going to kill you; you wait." I lifted the handle of the long locker that held our street clothes. We were supposed to keep our gym stuff in a permanent little locker and put our street clothes in one of the longer lockers set at intervals around the locker room, using the combination lock from our regular gym locker. Because we all despised dressing out and taking showers and never had enough time, most of us simply set our combination lock on the last number so all we had to do was touch it and it would open. I opened the door, my gymsuit already unbuttoned and hanging around my hips. The locker was empty.

"Where are our clothes?" I screamed. "Did you put the lock on the wrong locker?"

Sandy peered into the empty locker, as if our clothes might have shrunk and were lurking in one of the dusty corners. "I put the lock on *this* locker! Kobie, what are we going to do? The bell is going to ring in three minutes!"

"Tell me about it! Our clothes have to be here somewhere," I said. "You take that side. Hurry up! My bus driver doesn't wait one second after the bell."

We ran through the locker room, yanking open empty lockers and slamming the metal doors when we didn't see our clothes. At last I found our stuff shoved in an unused gym locker.

"Here they are!" I cried to Sandy. I jumped into my skirt just as the bell shrilled, without even taking off my gymsuit, and buttoned my blouse up crookedly over the lumpy suit wadded around my waist. Sandy threw on her dress and stamped into her loafers. I crammed my pantyhose in my purse as we ran out of the locker room and across the lawn to the train of buses.

"Jeanette did this," I panted to Sandy. "If you hadn't opened your big mouth. . . ."

I made it to my bus just as the driver was closing the door and saw Sandy climb on the bus in front of mine. This little stunt was Jeanette's revenge, all right. I knew she'd find a way to get back at Sandy. That was her style. But what bothered me was why Jeanette felt it necessary to hide *my* clothes along with Sandy's, when it was Sandy who had gotten her in trouble.

Chapter 6

"If we go see Mr. Richards, we'll get out of first period," Sandy said one morning in homeroom. "He'll give us a pass. He's real nice. You'll like him."

The thought of getting out of first period English was tempting. All I'd be missing would be another sleep-inducing session of *The Merchant of Venice*. Next to art, English was normally my favorite subject. But Mrs. Ragsdale's timid little voice and rabbity gestures took all the punch out of what was supposed to be a very powerful drama.

"I don't know," I told Sandy. "Guidance counselors in this school must be awfully busy. Don't we have to make an appointment or something?"

"No, you just walk in. I've been to see him a whole bunch of times already. He'll help us straighten out this thing with Jeanette; you'll see."

If Mr. Richards, who sounded like a cross between Santa Claus and Albert Schweitzer, was as wonderful as she claimed he was, then our troubles with Jeanette Adams would soon be over.

Jeanette had not stopped at hiding our clothes just once for kicks. Two or three times a week, Sandy and I came in from the field, sweaty and panting, to find our clothes missing. We complained to our teacher, Ms. Birmingham, and she made a speech in front of the class, but that didn't do any good. The culprit wasn't in our *class*, it was the one person who never dressed out and who spent gym period either sitting on the bleachers trying to look frail or skulking around the locker room, devising new ways for Kobie and Sandy to play Beat the Clock, when we were all outside on the field.

Yesterday, the clock nearly won. Sandy and I were in danger of having to wear our gymsuits home on the bus or spending the night in the locker room, because Jeanette had hidden our clothes in the towel room. But I found them in time, barely, and vowed to Sandy as we sprinted for the buses that I wasn't going to take this anymore. Making matters worse, Sandy had lost our combination lock so there was nothing to prevent Jeanette from hiding our clothes every day, if she wanted.

This morning when I arrived in homeroom, Sandy suggested going to our guidance counselor, since we shared everything in this school but the same desks.

"Jeanette's gotten away with murder long enough," Sandy said. "Remember the first time she took our clothes? I forgot to get my clunky shoes from our main locker. I went home in my loafers and my mother hit the ceiling. She told me if she caught me wearing regular shoes again she'd tan my hide." As Sandy spoke, she snapped her gum and jauntily swung one nonorthopedic-loafered foot. Apparently her mother's threats, like Mrs. Benson's halfhearted attempts to make the class stop chewing gum, didn't bother her much.

"If you really think it'll do some good," I said, weakening. "Ms. Birmingham doesn't listen when we tell her what's going on. Why should Mr. Richards be any different?"

"He helped me with my schedule," Sandy said. "They put me back in remedial math, but Mr. Richards transferred me to this other special class. He's great."

"All right," I agreed. "We'll go see your wonderful Mr. Richards."

When the bell rang, we went to the office instead of our first-period classes. Sandy breezed through the door, while I lagged behind. No one challenged us. In fact, no one even looked at us. The office was jam-packed with students slouched on the cracked vinyl couches or staring at the bulletin boards, wearing blank expressions. I knew that look. They were probably kids in trouble, candidates for detention or suspension or worse, with their faces arranged to show they didn't care. Not surprisingly, a school as big and overcrowded as Woodson meant that the office waiting room was usually full.

What *was* surprising was that I seldom — make that never — saw anyone of authority out in the halls, patrolling and cruising, the way the vice-principal did at Robert Frost. I knew that besides the principal, there were three vice-principals, plus squads of other administrative people, but they either existed in name and title only or were too scared to come out of their offices.

Mr. Richards was in his cubicle on guidance counselor row and, unlike his fellow advisers, he had left his door open.

"Come in, come in," he said when he saw us hesitating in the doorway. "Sandy Robertson, you've brought a friend."

Giggling, Sandy sat down in one of two chairs pulled up to his desk. "This is Kobie Roberts."

"Roberts and Robertson," Mr. Richards observed. "How interesting. Can I do something for you ladies today or is this a social visit?"

"No, we came on business," Sandy said.

"And here I thought you came just to see me." Mr. Richards sounded truly disappointed. He was a nice-looking man with coal black hair and dark eyes behind black-rimmed glasses.

"Actually," Sandy began, "Kobie wanted to see you."

I stared at her in amazement. Wasn't it *her* idea to come here and settle *our* problem? What was this "Kobie wanted to see you" business?

Mr. Richards turned to me. "What seems to be the problem, Kobie?"

Where did I start? With Jeanette causing me grief in home ec and gym, or Miss Channing blaming every little class disturbance on me? Or the crowded halls, or the upperclassmen who treated freshmen like dirt, or never being able to find a seat in the cafeteria?

"This school . . ." I said at last.

"What about this school?" Mr. Richards prompted.

"It's driving me crazy."

He laughed. "I know the feeling! Well, the situation here is unusual. Woodson was designed to accommodate twenty-five hundred students, and this year we have almost four thousand."

"Four thousand!" Sandy and I exclaimed together. No wonder we had classes in the halls and in Quonset huts — we should feel lucky not to have classes on the roof!

With Mr. Richards' encouragement, I selected the two most pressing problems out of my bag of grumbles and told him about Miss Channing and Jeanette. He listened, although he checked his watch periodically. It was rather warm in the little office, so when I finished, he unbuttoned the cuffs of his white shirt and began rolling his sleeves.

"You have to realize Miss Channing is somewhat set in her ways," Mr. Richards said. "She's been with the school system a long time. In her day, she was a very good teacher. She was given a chance to retire this year, but she wanted to continue teaching. I think the overcrowded conditions have thrown her off stride a little. We're all busy here."

I barely heard a thing he said. Instead I was fascinated by the sudden appearance of Mr. Richards' arms. Beneath the rolled-up sleeves of his dazzlingly white shirt, his forearms were muscled, tanned, and very, very, *very* hairy. He looked as if he were wearing a gorilla suit under his regular clothes. I tried not to stare but like most things you aren't supposed to stare at, I couldn't lift my eyes from those arms.

". . . continue to have problems with this girl, let me know. But make sure you go through proper channels, Kobie. You should discuss this first with your P.E. teacher." I wondered what he did when the moon got full.

Sandy started to laugh, a sputtery, muffled giggle. I knew she was thinking what I was thinking. Mr. Richards, the wolf man.

"Communication is the key," he went on, ignoring her outburst. "I'm glad you girls came here today. I want you to feel you can stop in any time." Despite his words, that was a definite dismissal. Mr. Richards crossed his arms, and they looked even darker and furrier against the white of his shirtfront. Sandy's giggling was getting out of control. "Is something funny, Sandy?" he finally asked her.

She avoided his eyes. "No, sir. I — I just remembered a joke my father told me."

"Do you want to let us in on it?" Mr. Richards said.

That was too much for me. I began laughing, too, and couldn't stop. I held my hand over my mouth, but all that did was make my nose run. If I didn't get out of his office and away from the sight of those hairy arms, I was going to do something disgraceful.

"Well," I said, standing up. "Thank you for your time, Mr. uh — " What was the man's *name*? Wasn't it like a boy's name? " — Mr. Hairy!" I finished brilliantly.

I couldn't run out fast enough.

Behind my bedroom door, my father was making strange grunting sounds interspersed with a few swearwords as he laid my new purple carpet. The carpeting had actually arrived sometime before, but the carpet store people had only installed the wall-to-wall stuff, leaving us to put down the room-size remnant ourselves. Dad had been working overtime a lot lately, and on his first free Saturday he had promised to lay my carpet. Well, that Saturday was here, but my father was less than delighted with all the junk on my floor. I tossed everything on my bed. The mattress sagged under the weight, and I worried the box springs wouldn't hold. Then we dragged my furniture out into the hall, except for my bed, which Dad said he'd work around. My mother and I volunteered to assist with the carpet, but my father claimed we were always standing on the part of the rug he wanted to unroll and he'd rather do it himself.

While Dad was in my room alternately grunting and cussing, I decided it was a good time to talk to my mother. Hadn't Mr. Richards said communication was the key? Maybe my mother would come up with a solution for dealing with Jeanette, otherwise known as the Kiss of Death.

My mother was in her room, adding up a long column of numbers on the back of an old envelope.

I immediately got the discussion off on the wrong foot. "Do you think it's necessary to know how to cook?" I wanted to tell her that high school wasn't turning out to be the big adventure I thought it was going to be, and that was what came out. Cooking!

"Of course," Mom murmured, erasing a number. "Everybody should learn how to cook."

"But is it *essential*, like English or history?"

"No, but as long as they offer it in school, you might as well take it and do the best you can. Someday you may get married, Kobie, and your husband will probably expect you to know how to cook. That's not an unreasonable demand, even in this day and age."

"But what if I'm a famous animator for Walt Disney Studios," I said. "It really wouldn't *matter* if I could cook or not."

"I suppose not, but it's hard to eat cartoons. You should think of your husband and children. Other people will be depending on you."

She had a point. I pictured myself married to some faceless, nameless man who would have a meager supper of watery tomato soup and burned cheese sandwiches. Of course, he could make supper, too.

I didn't really want to talk about cooking. I wanted to tell my mother how rough high school was and what an awful year I was having, thanks to a certain tough girl. Maybe she'd offer to go to Woodson and have Jeanette arrested or something. But Mom kept adding and re-adding that column of numbers.

She sighed. "It always comes out the same. Not enough."

"Not enough what?"

"Never mind, Miss Nosy."

Dad came out then, perspiring mightily, and began hauling my furniture back inside. When he was through, I squealed at the sight of my new room. The royal purple carpet made it look bigger, and my old furniture didn't seem quite so shabby.

"Doesn't it look terrific?" I asked my mother.

Her eyes arrowed to the junk heaped on my bed. "I want all that stuff put away and put away right — *not* crammed under the bed."

"Aw, Mom! I was going to draw this afternoon. Can't I do that later?"

My mother still had the envelope of numbers in her hand. She waved it angrily under my nose. "You promised me you'd clean up your room if I bought you that rug. If you weren't planning to keep your promise, I could have saved us some money. But, no, you had to make a fool of yourself in the carpet store. Well, you got your rug, Kobie Roberts, and you're going to clean up this rat's nest if it takes forever. Now get busy!"

I walked very slowly over to my bed and picked the first item off the pile, one of my recent drawings. While my mother glared at me, I opened the bottom drawer of my bureau and very slowly laid the drawing inside. Still in slow motion, I went back to the bed and picked up the next item. I planned to make cleaning up my room last forever, just as she ordered.

"Kobie, are you mocking me?" my mother demanded.

"I'm doing exactly what you *told* me. Cleaning my room." I stared back at her, a pair of ripped underpants in my hand. It isn't easy staring down your mother holding a pair of torn underpants, but I stood my ground. She hadn't said one thing about how nice my room looked with the purple rug. All she could see was the mess on my bed. That's all she *ever* saw.

She returned my stare, measure for measure, then left without another word. I didn't know what was bugging my mother lately. Sometimes she acted okay, but other times it was as if we were enemies.

I remembered once, when I was six, I was watching Popeye on TV while sucking on a marble. I accidentally swallowed the marble, and it scared me so bad, I ran, choking and making pointing motions at my throat, to the kitchen where my mother was ironing.

"What's wrong with you?" my mother screamed, alarmed. "Tell me!"

"I 'wallowed a 'arble," I managed to get out and then began to bawl.

"Oh, Kobie!" My mother hustled me through the living room, back to the bathroom. Just as we reached the threshold, I threw up, splashing vomit all over the waxed hardwood floor. One more step and I would have been in the bathroom where the floor was tiled. Two more steps and I would have been over the toilet bowl.

My mother put me to bed with my favorite bunny tucked beside me, and then, after she had mopped up the mess and realized I wasn't going to die, yelled at me, "Why couldn't you have thrown up in the toilet!"

That was the way things had been with us lately. I knew my mother loved me, but she never really *talked* to me, only criticized. It was as if she was still finding fault with me for not making it to the toilet in time.

Chapter 7

November sixth, the last day of our eight-week grading period, should go down in history for two remarkable incidents. It was the day that Marianne Andrews gave me the first sign she might want to be friends. It was also the day I gave myself a mohawk. I would like to believe the two events were directly related, because the only other explanation for what happened at Gretchen's is that I lost my mind.

As I skidded into geography class a whole three minutes before the bell, I noticed Marianne Andrews perched on Mr. Eaton's desk, the center of attention. She had cut off her long, beautiful hair and gotten one of those daring geometric cuts. Like everyone else, I stopped to stare at her. The new cut was a shock, but she looked even more breathtaking, more dramatic.

Mr. Eaton was sitting at Marianne's

desk, laughing at something she had just said. "Now you won't feel compelled to cut off your split ends every day in my class."

Without thinking, I said, "She didn't really have split ends. Marianne's hair is much too pretty to have ugly old split ends like the rest of us."

Then I realized that I had actually spoken to the leader of the elite group I had been admiring from afar all year. Marianne turned her full attention on me, and I suddenly felt exposed, like a marauding raccoon caught in the beam of a searchlight.

"Have I seen you before?" she asked.

"Right here. I'm in this class," I replied, my palms slick.

"No, I mean someplace else."

"We have gym together." Of course she wouldn't remember seeing me in gym. She and Barbara Phillips were very athletic, while Sandy and I, poor at every game but tiddlywinks, were usually chosen last or stuck way out in left field, even when we *weren't* playing softball.

"What's your name?" the Great One asked me. I felt like Dorothy finally being granted an audience by the Wizard of Oz.

"Kobie Roberts." Maybe I should curtsy or shuffle my feet a little to let her know how thrilled I was to have her shining beacon settle on me, if only fleetingly.

"Well, Kobie, I'm taking a survey. Do you like my hair better long or short?"

Was this a trick question? If I answered one way and it was wrong would that condemn me in Marianne's eyes forever? I enjoyed basking in the warm glow of the inner circle and was reluctant to crawl back into the clammy dark pit of the unpopular.

"I loved your hair when it was long," I replied carefully. "But I love it short, too. You look sort of wild, like Peter Pan."

Marianne and Barbara, her underling, laughed.

"No, really," I added hastily. "You're one of those lucky people who can wear any hairstyle and look absolutely great."

Marianne rewarded me with a smile and I felt as if I had somehow been noticed, and was grateful to be allowed a glimpse into the magical realms of the right people.

"Kobie Roberts," Marianne said thoughtfully, weighing the sound of my name. I knew what she was thinking. She was wondering if she had overlooked me as a possible member of her clique. When Mr. Eaton called the class to order, I went to my seat, faint with elation.

There was a note on my desk. An invitation from Marianne already? I opened it eagerly but slumped with despair when I saw the familiar drawing of the White House. The words in the balloon over the roof read, "Shall we dine in the Blue Room or the Green Room this evening?" Air Force One trailed a banner bearing the message, "Want me to save you a place at lunch today?"

I hadn't seen Eddie Showalter in the cafeteria since the day Stuart Buckley had borrowed fifty cents from me, although I admit I had looked around for Eddie once or twice. But this was too much like — well, not exactly a date, but certainly a big deal. Saving seats at lunch led to sharing lockers and other boy/girl stuff. Not that I wouldn't mind the company of a cute boy. But now that I was being considered for Marianne's group, it would never do to be seen with an obvious loser like Eddie Showalter.

No, thanks, I printed firmly at the bottom of the note. Then I scribbled, to soften the blow and satisfy my own curiosity, *How come you always draw the White House?*

I could tell Eddie was disappointed I had turned him down, but he scribbled a reply and handed the note back to me.

That's where I'm going to live. Didn't you know I'm going to wind up in the White House?

He planned to be President! More likely

he'll wind up in a padded cell at St. Elizabeth's, the local mental hospital. I put the note in my geography book, intending to throw it away as soon as I could. Eddie Showalter was an even bigger loser than I had originally thought. Turning him off was the smartest thing I had done all day.

So it was only natural that I followed such a decisive act with the stupidest thing I have done in *years*.

After school I went over to Gretchen's house. The evening started off uneventfully. Mrs. Farris made corned beef hash and canned peas for supper, catering to my Friday night habit. Instead of cream soda, though, we had apple juice. Gretchen had read in a fan magazine that a member of our favorite rock group, the Byrds, drank apple juice. She was always gleaning tidbits from *Hit Parade* and *Tiger Beat*, and if a rock star said he liked apple juice and some obscure Greek actress, then *we* drank apple juice and watched her old movies on the late show.

I didn't really like the apple juice: It tasted like water flavored with yellow crayon, and I was glad we didn't have to suffer through any boring old Greek movies.

We went to Gretchen's room after we ate. I flopped down on her bed and began thumbing through a stack of magazines on her nightstand. Gretchen put her newest album on the record player, and we settled in for a long, uninterrupted chat.

"Kobie, it's been ages since we've really talked — "

"Look at the great stuff in here," I said, paging through the Sears Wishbook Christmas catalog. "How come they come up with all these neat toys after we're too old for them?"

"You want a new Barbie for Christmas?" Gretchen teased. "Speaking of which, what're you asking for?"

Like most red-blooded American kids, I make a Christmas "Want" list. Usually I begin the list sometime around October and add to it and add to it in a white heat of anticipation, only to have to slash it to a few hundred vital items, the first fifty starred as "must haves." But here it was November and I hadn't even thought of starting my list yet.

"I could just hand Mom my right things list," I said. "And put 'can't live without' next to every item. Knowing my mother, she's already bought me something for Christmas like days-of-the-week underwear.

"You know," I said, shoving the catalog away, "I never got a chemistry set and I asked for one every single year. Mom always made some limp excuse like, 'Santa

Claus can't deliver chemistry sets' or 'They're too dangerous,' and dumb me believed her. She never *wanted* me to have a chemistry set, just like she doesn't want me to have my room the way I like it or look the way I ought to."

Gretchen sat on the bed and picked up the latest issue of *Seventeen*. "She did get you a new carpet, Kobie. You can't complain about that."

I didn't like Gretchen siding with my mother, even indirectly. She was *my* mother, and if I wanted to dredge up old slights, like being deprived of a chemistry set for Christmas, then Gretchen should sympathize with me. Anyhow, Gretchen was a good one to talk. Last year, before she got home from the hospital, her mother had gone out and bought a new bedspread and curtains for her room. I was dying for a turquoise bedspread and lime-green curtains to go with my purple rug, but do you think my mother would take an interest in her only child's bedroom, the place where her daughter spent one third of her life? No, she thought the purple carpet was enough. I loved my rug, but without the turquoise and lime-green accents to balance all that purple, it was like living in a giant bowl of blueberries.

"Listen," Gretchen said. "I need to talk to you about — "

"Mom won't get me anything on my right things list," I grumbled. "I can't seem to get through to her that life at Woodson isn't worth *living* without those things."

"You'd be surprised," Gretchen said quietly. "Life *with* those things isn't all that great either."

"What are you talking about?" I said. "You've got almost everything on our list. You don't have to worry about getting in the right group at Frost — you *are* the right group."

Gretchen put down her magazine to face me. "Is that what you think? Maybe you should come by Frost one day and see just how popular I am."

"I wouldn't set foot back in that stupid place if you paid me a million dollars."

Gretchen threw the magazine at me. "See what I mean! You have no idea what it's like being left back a grade or you wouldn't make cracks like that." She flounced off the bed and plumped down at her vanity table, her back toward me.

I ignored Gretchen's little flare-up, more interested in the *Seventeen* she had pitched at me. The magazine had fallen open to a page of hairstyles designed by Vidal Sassoon. A blonde girl with nonstop teeth modeled a short geometric haircut just like Marianne Andrews'.

"Look at this!" I cried, sliding off the bed with the magazine turned to the photograph. "Gretchen, what do you think of this haircut?"

Still miffed, she said, "You mean you're actually asking *my* opinion? I don't know, Kobie, it's awfully extreme. Her hair comes clear above her ears."

"It's supposed to. A girl in my geography class got her hair cut just like this and she looks terrific, not that she wasn't terrific-looking to start with." I was seized with a sudden inspiration. "Gretchen, I'm going to cut my hair!"

Gretchen's blue eyes widened. "When?"

"Now! Right this minute!"

"Oh, Kobie, you can't be serious! Cut your *hair*? Look at that hairstyle — you'd never be able to do that. Why don't you ask your mom to take you to Vincent and Vincent and get it done right?"

"If I wait until that day comes, I'll be old and gray. I have to do it now — tonight! Get me some scissors, quick, before I lose my nerve."

"No chance of that," Gretchen remarked sarcastically, but she got me a pair of scissors.

I wet my hair, combed it out straight, then grabbed the scissors. Gretchen acted as my assistant, setting up mirrors in order for me to view my hair from all angles and holding the magazine up so I could see the hairstyle better.

The first hank of hair fell to the newspapers we had spread around on the floor. I was committed. Recklessly, I hacked off my shoulder-length hair until it was just below my ears, then I began to shape it like the picture in the magazine. Or at least I tried to.

"One side's shorter than the other," Gretchen observed. "I'll get a razor and even it up."

She evened up one side but then the *other* side seemed crooked so we worked on that side, and before long I didn't have any sides left to even up. It was then I realized several things at once. I had forgotten to take into consideration the shrink factor — wet hair becomes shorter when dry. I had also forgotten to account for the curl factor — my hair didn't fall into smooth geometric lines but sprang up like Little Orphan Annie's hair. And lastly, I realized that short hair looked horrible on me.

I burst into tears. "Gretchen! What am I going to *do*! I look awful! I can't go home like this! I can't go *any*where looking like this!"

Gretchen mashed my microlocks down, trying to cover at least part of my endless forehead, but the curls kept springing up again. "It's not as bad as you think. Go home and work with it some. Maybe you can train it to lie down."

I looked at my reflection again, hoping that my hair had grown an inch or so since the last time I looked. "I couldn't get this stuff to lie down if you dropped a manhole cover on my head! Gretchen, I'm nearly *bald*!"

Mrs. Farris came in to see what all the carrying on was about. "Kobie! What have you done to your hair!"

"Ruined it!" I wailed.

Like the wonderful mother she was, Mrs. Farris patted my shoulder and said soothingly, "There, there, Kobie. Your mother will take you to Vincent and Vincent, and they can fix your hair. Don't cry. It'll be all right."

It wasn't all right. The minute I got home, I ran into my mother's room, flung myself across her bed, and demanded she drive me to the beauty parlor that very instant.

"Absolutely not," my mother said. "We can't afford an expensive salon like Vincent and Vincent. Can you imagine what they'd charge to straighten out a mess like yours? What possessed you to chop off your hair, Kobie?"

"I wanted to look like a model in *Seventeen*."

"You can't make a peach out of a pear," my mother said unhelpfully. She was famous for handing out platitudes whenever I was having a crisis.

"Gretchen's mother *said* you'd take me to Vincent and Vincent," I insisted.

"Gretchen's mother has nothing to do with this. You're *my* daughter."

"Sometimes I wish I weren't!"

"That makes two of us."

"Mom, you *have* to take me to Vincent and Vincent." I mustered up a few fake tears. "I can't go to school like this!"

"You can and you will. I know you, Kobie. You thought if you botched your hair I'd feel sorry for you and take you to the beauty parlor. I told you weeks ago when you were whining about wanting this and wanting that that we were tight on money. No beauty parlor."

I couldn't believe my own mother was being so mean! Hurling myself on my back, I yelled and thrashed my legs. When that didn't have any effect, I drummed my feet on the footboard of her bed. "You have to take me! You have to!"

"I don't *have* to do anything," my mother said coldly. "But if you want to get up from there and act your age, I'll see what I can do with your hair."

She was definitely not taking me to Vincent and Vincent. Burying my face in my father's pillow, I began to sob, but this time the tears were real. My mother was a worse haircutter than I was.

Chapter 8

I was in the doghouse the whole weekend. My mother spoke to me only when she absolutely had to. On Saturday I guiltily watched my father nail the footboard back into place. He said, "I'm disappointed in you, Kobie. Why do you give your mother such a hard time?"

"How come she gives *me* such a hard time?"

He didn't say anything for a few minutes, but when he did, it was to relay an order. "In the future when you use my razor, please have the decency to clean it out and put in a new blade. I almost cut my throat the other day."

"How do you know Mom isn't using your razor?" I hedged.

"Just do like I tell you."

There was no school on Monday, because of a teachers' workday, which gave me nearly forty-eight hours to grow my hair out. My mother evened up the back, covering the worst of my mistakes. "It'll grow," she said. Small comfort. My hair was still too short. I slept Monday night with Dippety-Do slathered all over my hair and an old pillowcase turbaned around my head to keep my hair flat and protect my bedclothes from the grease. The next day my hair had the plastered set look of a football helmet, but at least it was lying flat, and anything was a big improvement over Little Orphan Annie.

I expected everybody on the bus to die laughing, but when nobody did, I decided I could dye my hair green and those kids wouldn't notice, we'd been together so long.

"Does it look too awful?" I asked Gretchen.

"No. It looks okay." She stared glumly out the window.

"What's *your* problem? *I'm* the one who has to go to school bald."

"Nothing, Kobie. Forget it."

I was in no mood for her little games. "Pardon me for living." We didn't talk the rest of the way to Woodson.

I got to the locker before Sandy, hoping she had left a spare paper bag in it. I wanted to put one over my head and pretend I was left over from Halloween. Maybe I was going overboard, as my mother said. No one would pay any attention to my haircut if —

"Hey, Kobie!" The loudest voice in the entire universe boomeranged around the corner and down the hall. "What happened to *you*! Get your head caught in a fan?" Naturally, people stopped to stare at me.

Stuart Buckley, owner of that big mouth, bounced through the crowd and scampered over to my locker.

"How much, Stuart?" I said before he could ask.

"A dollar, if you've got it. Anything you can spare. Although looking at that hairdo, I don't think you can spare much."

"Keep your wisecracks to yourself." I gave him a quarter, the only extra change I had. "Stuart, this is the third time in two weeks you've borrowed money from me. What's going on?"

Stuart edged closer to my locker, reminding me of all those times I wanted to push him into the locker, slam the door, and throw away the key. "Promise you won't tell?" I agreed. "There's this guy who makes me give him money or else he'll beat me up. That's why I need the cash."

"What?" I was outraged. "You mean you pay some big bully so he won't hit you? Why don't you go to the principal or somebody?"

Stuart curled his lip in disgust. It was the same look my father wore whenever he talked about the scarcity of policemen on the Beltway during rush hour. "You *are* kidding, aren't you?" Stuart said. "Got to run. See you around, Kobie."

In homeroom, Sandy made a big fuss over my hair, saying how much she liked it. She was proudly wearing a cheap circle pin on the round collar of her shirt. "Just like on your right things list," she told me.

Well, not exactly. There was a certain way to wear circle pins and they only looked good on certain collars. Sandy's collar was too floppy, not neat like Marianne's and Barbara's, and her shirt was wrinkled, as if she had slept in her clothes under an old tarpaulin. Sandy was one of those unfortunate people who, even when wearing the best outfits, always looked like she dressed herself with a pitchfork. But since she was nice about my hair, I told her she looked "just right."

First period went okay. What I was really dreading was third period, when Marianne Andrews would see my awful haircut. I knew she would know I was trying to copy *her*, and that the terrible result was only what I deserved for brashly thinking I was good enough for her group. Despite Sandy's reassurance (and here I had to consider the source), my spirits were rock-bottom when I scuffed into second period home ec.

Sandy was waiting for me in the test kitchen. Jeanette was late, but that was nothing earthshaking. She'd flaunt her forged pass and Miss Channing would let her in, smiling her Betty Crocker smile. If I had my way, I'd give Jeanette a pass that would not only excuse her from all her classes, but from this planet as well. Jeanette hadn't hidden our clothes recently in gym, so I should have been thankful.

Miss Channing had demonstrated making doughnuts last week and that was what we were doing today. For once we had an actual recipe in our hands, but as part of our assignment we were supposed to either double or halve the ingredients. What with the hectic haircutting episode, I had forgotten which, if I had ever known.

"I can't do fractions," Sandy admitted. "Do we go up or down?"

"I don't know. If we ask Miss Channing, she'll put a big black mark in her gradebook for not listening in class." I tore the ditto sheet in two and gave the top part to Sandy. "You work on these and I'll do the rest."

We were both so feeble in arithmetic that it took us nearly half of the period to figure the fractions. By the time we were finished, Jeanette waltzed in, slinging her purse on the dinette table.

"Wow! Look at you! What happened to your *hair*!"

"She had it cut," Sandy said, which was not quite the truth. "I think it's real cute. Kobie looks like — Lassie!"

"Thanks a lot," I told her sourly.

Jeanette hooted. "Kobie looks like a dog, all right!"

Sandy got out the big mixing bowl. "Don't you think Lassie is cute? I wouldn't mind looking like a collie. They're so soft and fluffy." So was Sandy's brain, but that would be overstating the obvious.

"What's Lassie fixing today?" With iridescent liner, Jeanette striped her eyelids.

I ignored her and busied myself gathering the ingredients for the doughnuts.

"I hope these doughnuts don't turn out like that banana cream pie," Jeanette remarked. "That pie would have gagged a maggot."

"Well," I said, "it certainly gagged *you*."

Jeanette nailed me with one of her steel-melting looks. "You calling me a maggot, girl?"

"Of course not. I was merely agreeing with you about the pie." My heart tripped over itself as it sped up. My haircut must have made me light-headed, to be talking to Jeanette Adams that way!

"It was terrible," Sandy put in quickly. She may have been a fluff-brain, but she recognized that dangerous tone in Jeanette's voice. "Our doughnuts will be better. We've got a recipe today. You can have the first one, Jeanette."

"I'm not that brave," Jeanette muttered, but she stopped picking on me and settled into her familiar routine, telling us about her boyfriend the Viper and putting on her makeup.

I often wondered what spell Jeanette had cast over Miss Channing. She didn't do anything in class except run her mouth and make fun of Miss Channing, calling her "that old windbag" and "the old dragon" practically to her face. On our cooking days she sat at the dinette table like the Queen of Sheba, in full view of the class, and anyone not legally blind could see that she never did a speck of work in the kitchen.

"How does she get away with it?" I whispered to Sandy. "Miss Channing acts stranger than ever when Jeanette's around."

"Jeanette butters her up. Haven't you heard when she comes in late? She always compliments Miss Channing on her dress or tells her that her hair looks pretty."

So that was Jeanette's secret, at least with Miss Channing. In gym class, her method was to wimp around the locker room until Ms. Birmingham was out of sight and then she'd snap back to her regular rotten self. Ms. Birmingham was not the type to fall for idle flattery, but she did honor Jeanette's fake doctor's note, though I suspected the teacher knew it was a phony.

Sandy measured the ingredients from her half of the ditto sheet, then I dumped in mine. Soon we had a platter piled high with delicious-looking doughnuts.

As Sandy dipped the boiling hot doughnuts in confectioner's sugar, I made a stab at cleaning up some of the mess. I checked Sandy's half of the ingredients list. I had *halved* the milk, sugar, and eggs, while she had *doubled* the amount of cinnamon, shortening, flour, and salt. As usual, we were working at cross-purposes. I could imagine what those doughnuts would taste like.

Miss Channing came in. Our powdered doughnuts were heaped invitingly on a platter, but she didn't dare sample one. Instead, she picked up a doughnut, held her arm out stiffly, and let it drop. The doughnut hit the table like a slug of plutonium.

"Bit heavy," Miss Channing pronounced,

jotting in her ever-present gradebook. I
longed to wrest that infernal gradebook
away from her and dash down to the fur-
nace room to toss it into the flames.

"Okay, girls," she said to us. "Enjoy
your snack."

Actually, the doughnuts were pretty
good. They were a little gummy from
Sandy's putting the confectioner's sugar
on while they were still hot and somewhat
heavy, but that didn't stop Sandy from
eating seven and me from downing nine.
The doughnuts made our hands unusually
greasy, and we had to keep getting clean
paper napkins.

A few minutes before the bell, Jeanette
packed up her satchel and sneaked out of
class while Miss Channing had her back
turned. That was her latest ploy: sneaking
out early to go to the girls' room. I don't
know why she needed to go there — home
ec was like one great big girls' room to her.
Sandy and I kept on eating, lost in a
doughnut Shangri-la.

When the bell rang, jerking us from our
binge, we still had to clean the kitchen. I
grabbed the now-empty platter and tried
to jump up, but my feet seemed cemented
to the floor.

Sandy clutched her middle. "My stomach
hurts!"

Sharp pains darted through my midsection. "Mine, too. It must be all that grease. You doubled the shortening, remember?"

Lurching around the kitchen, we managed to wipe up the spilled sugar and flour, but I felt just like the time I had swallowed a marble, only worse. I pictured those doughnuts forming a solid ball in my stomach and trying to break loose, like a boat tethered to a dock during a storm.

I was late to third period. I entered the class listing heavily to the left, which was where the doughnut-ball had lodged itself temporarily. Mr. Eaton accepted my excuse about having to clean up in home ec and said nothing about my odd walk as I staggered to my desk. Eddie Showalter watched my unsteady progress, probably afraid I'd topple out of my seat and land on him. My doughnut ballast shifted to the right.

Just as Mr. Eaton was about to start the day's lesson, Sandy's face appeared around the edge of the blackboard that served as a room partition. I stumbled to the front to see what she wanted.

"You forgot your geography book," Sandy said. "Here."

"Thanks." I clasped the book to my stomach. Even that slight motion was like thumping a bass drum. "Do you feel as bad as I do?"

She nodded. "I can hardly walk. I hope

this stuff wears off fast. We'll never be able to run in gym."

I felt eyes boring in my back. Turning, I saw Marianne Andrews and Barbara Phillips point to Sandy's collar. Marianne gave me a smirk. Sandy looked around me, recognized Marianne and Barbara from gym class, and waved cheerfully. Marianne waggled her fingers in return.

"Well, I gotta go," Sandy chirped. "See you guys later!"

"Oh, yeah," Barbara drawled. "You'll see us, all right."

As I wobbled back to my seat, I heard Barbara comment to Marianne, "Did you see her pin! That collar!" They giggled like fiends.

My face burned. I knew they were making fun of Sandy. I was embarrassed for Sandy, but I was also ashamed to have been seen with her. I still wanted to get into Marianne's group. I might have a chance, but I couldn't afford any liabilities, and that meant Sandy Robertson.

Chapter 9

Report card day at W.T. Woodson had all the excitement of an execution. The normally clogged and noisy hallways were subdued, as if we all moved under a cloud of doom. Kids laughed and joked as usual, but the laughter seemed distracted and abrupt. I could almost see their gloomy worries etched over their heads like words in a cartoon balloon: "Will I pass English?" "If I don't get at least a C in math...."

At Robert Frost Intermediate, students were handed a brown envelope in homeroom. The envelope contained six cards, one for each subject. The same cards were used for every reporting period, which meant that we couldn't throw them away or hide them from our parents, since the cards had to be signed and turned back in.

I sat nervously at my desk in homeroom,

waiting for the ax to fall. Mrs. Benson was fooling around with a pile of thin papers. Behind me, Sandy jiggled her foot and hummed.

Cheryl Ramsey turned around to speak to me. "This is the worst part of the whole year! What's taking her so *long*? Doesn't she know we're dying?"

"She knows," I said. "She just likes to watch us squirm."

At last Mrs. Benson began calling the roll. But instead of distributing brown envelopes when she was finished, she had each one of us come up to her desk as she read our names.

"Is that our report card?" I asked Cheryl, as the first kid returned to his seat clutching a small slip of paper.

Cheryl shrugged. "Beats me. Looks like a piece of toilet paper to me."

"Roberts, Kobie," Mrs. Benson said. I walked up to her desk with shaking knees. She picked up the next slip of paper from the stack on the corner of her desk, checked to make sure it was mine, then gave it to me without comment.

I studied the paper, which was a computer-printed slip and difficult to interpret. Subjects were abbreviated. "09 HPE Girls" turned out to be ninth-grade girls' gym. Why couldn't they just *say* "girls' gym"? The next column listed my teachers by last name and the next column, the most important one, finally stated my grades.

My heart dropped like the doughnuts Sandy and I had made. I had gotten four A's, a D, and an *F*! F as in *Failure*! The A's were in my academic subjects and the D in gym, so it didn't take any great brain to figure out what the F was in. Miss Channing strikes again.

I whipped around in my chair. "Sandy! Channing gave me an F!"

"I got one, too," she said. "Plus an F in gym and D's in everything but English! When my mother sees this report card, she's going to smash all my records! She won't let me watch TV for six months! She'll probably ground me at least a month. What's your mother going to do to you, Kobie?"

I moaned. "Sandy, I can't take this report card home! I've never gotten an F in my entire life! She can't do this to me!"

"Did you get any comments?"

"What?"

"Give me your report card." I passed it back to her. She whistled at the sight of my A's. I guess to her they did look impressive, but all I could see was that big fat F at the top, blocking the glory of my A's. Sandy indicated a row of numbers under the "Comments" heading. "Channing gave you the same numbers she did me."

I stared at the last column. "What do they mean?"

"You have to look them up on the back."

Channing had given me a one, a three, and a five. All odd. I remembered the first day of school when she divided the class into groups of four, then reached our table, where there were only three of us. The odd bunch, she had called us. The comments key on the back said that I needed to use time more wisely, to form better work habits, and to develop a more cooperative attitude! In addition to the numbers, an asterisk indicated Miss Channing requested a conference. With whom, I didn't know. I'd like to have a private conference and tell her what I thought of *her*!

Sandy got a one, three, and five, too. I was incensed.

"What's the matter with that stupid woman?" I ranted. "We've done everything in that class except lick the floors, and she says we're not cooperative! I wonder what Jeanette got on *her* report card. You can bet it wasn't an F!"

Jeanette was in a sullen mood in home ec. She showed us her report card only after we showed her ours. She narrowed her eyes at my row of A's, but said nothing. When she slid her report card across the table, I pounced on it.

"A *C*!" I whispered hotly to Sandy. "The Wicked Witch of the West gave Jeanette a C! There is no justice in this world!"

"It isn't fair," Sandy said. "Let's go see Mr. Richards."

After our last disastrous visit, I wasn't exactly champing at the bit to see our guidance counselor again. But I needed help, and he was the only person who could help me.

Mr. Richards seemed very harried. Dispensing with pleasantries, he asked us what the trouble was. I showed him our report cards. He didn't seem overly surprised by Sandy's marks, but my report card made him glance up at me with a curious expression.

"A rather mixed bag of grades, Kobie," he said. "You seem to have trouble in activity-related classes."

"I have trouble in Jeanette-related classes," I told him bluntly. "That girl will be the death of me. It's all her fault I got that D in gym and the F in home ec!"

"And how is that?" Mr. Richards wanted to know.

"See, in gym, Jeanette hides our clothes — mine and Sandy's — so that we never take showers like we're supposed to because we're always running around trying to find our stuff," I explained. "Ms. Birmingham grades down for not dressing out properly. And Miss Channing — well, who knows how *her* mind works. I've told you how Jeanette talks in class and never lifts a toenail to help in the kitchen. Yet Miss Channing gave her a C. Now, is that fair?"

Mr. Richards tapped a pencil on his blotter. To my everlasting relief, he kept his sleeves buttoned, and only a few stray hairs showed from beneath his shirt cuffs. "I can see how this *seems* unfair to you, Kobie, but I'm not sure that's the case. Miss Channing backs up her reasoning for the grade by the comments she listed. What's more, she requests a conference. How do you feel about your mother coming in to speak to Miss Channing?"

The same way I felt about electing Jeanette Adams Miss America — it was a preposterous suggestion. I shook my head. "My mother will never understand this in a million years. She'll take one look at that F and it'll be all over for me. You can forget any conference."

"Why do you say that?"

"Because I know my mother. She only sees the bad — she'll jump to the conclusion that it's my fault. That I must be a troublemaker to get such a bad grade. I've tried to tell her how horrible it's been this year, but she doesn't care." Tears welled up in my eyes. I *was* having a horrible year and the F proved it.

Mr. Richards hid a smile. "Are you having a terrible year, too?" he asked Sandy.

"Not really," she said amiably. "My report card is always bad. Kobie and I are friends, which helps a lot. I'd be awful lonesome without Kobie."

"Yes," he agreed. "I bet you would."

I looked at Sandy. "I thought you said your mother will kill you over your report card."

"She will. She always does." Sandy was so unruffled I wanted to throttle her. She was *used* to getting rotten grades.

"How can you be so calm? And why are we here if you don't care?" I asked her.

She shrugged. "I don't think you deserved an F."

And she did? That girl made no sense sometimes.

Mr. Richards directed the conversation back to me. "Kobie, you seem to be dumping all the blame on Jeanette Adams."

"Because it *is* her fault! Who *else* should I dump the blame on?" I demanded.

"I did some checking into Jeanette's records," Mr. Richards said. "Even though she's not one of the students I'm supposed to advise."

"What did you find out?" I was hoping he'd tell me she was on parole and would have to go back to jail, where she belonged.

"Well, I can't tell you everything, except that Miss Adams has quite a skip record. If she's caught skipping again, she'll be suspended."

A lot of good *that* would do. Like most kids who skipped, Jeanette obviously didn't want to be in school. In the school system's infinite wisdom, the punishment for skipping was a three-day suspension, in which the student was not *allowed* to come back to school.

"I wish she'd just drop out," I muttered. "She must be old enough — she makes two of me and Sandy."

"Jeanette *is* older than you and Sandy," Mr. Richards said, "but we discourage students from dropping out. It's our responsibility to see that everyone receives an education."

"Even at the expense of another student's education?" I couldn't believe I was actually talking to a grown-up this way.

But Mr. Richards was cool. He'd probably heard worse from kids like Jeanette. "You say Jeanette talks all the time in class. Does she talk about anything in particular?"

"Her boyfriend," Sandy replied. "And all the stuff her mother lets her do."

Mr. Richards made a tent of his hands.

"Now, that's interesting. Jeanette's mother is not living with the family and hasn't for some years."

"Where is she?" I asked, thinking if I had a kid like Jeanette I'd split, too.

"The whereabouts of Jeanette's mother is not the issue. What *is* important is that Jeanette talks about her mother as if she were still with the family. So you see, Kobie, even girls like Jeanette have problems." He stood up, indicating our meeting was finished.

If he was trying to make me feel sorry for Jeanette Adams, it wasn't working. Jeanette didn't have a mother, Stuart Buckley's stepmother was mean to him, Sandy limped because she once had polio. Why was it all the losers and rejects in the world clung to me like barnacles?

"Some help he was," I remarked witheringly. "Mr. Richards is just like all the rest of them. They pretend to be interested, but they really aren't. He's just collecting a salary like everybody else."

After school, I slinked into my house, trying not to alert my mother, who had report card radar. From the kitchen doorway, I saw she was occupied on the laundry porch, repotting her African violets.

Throwing my books on the sofa, I ran to call Gretchen.

"I got an F on my report card!" I

screeched as soon as the phone on the other end was picked up. "Oh, Mrs. Farris. I didn't mean to yell in your ear. Is Gretchen there?"

When Gretchen came on the line, I told her about my awful grades. "What am I going to do? You know my mother. She'll *kill* me!"

"You can't do anything," Gretchen replied dryly, "except show her your report card. You have to; she has to sign it."

"Only after she signs my death warrant! Gretchen, this is the worst thing to happen to me in my whole life! I hate Woodson! I hate being a freshman!"

"Kobie, do you think you're the first person in the world who's ever gotten a crummy report card?"

"Gretchen! I thought you were my *friend!*" I cried into the receiver. "You're supposed to sympathize with me!"

"Did you sympathize with me last year when I got all those incompletes on *my* report card?"

I wasn't sure what she was talking about for a second. Then I remembered she had been out of school many weeks, recovering from her accident. "This isn't the same thing. Your folks expected you to get a bad report card that time. You weren't in school."

"Grow up, Kobie. Nobody *expects* to get

a bad report card. Did you think that was a joyous occasion in my house? You're carrying on like you invented failing grades. You don't need to tell *me* about F's and D's — I'm an expert on the subject."

This was hardly the reaction I'd anticipated from my best friend. "What are *you* getting so upset about? Sure, you have to repeat eighth grade this year, but at least you've got nice clothes and a decent school. At least you're not bald!"

"You did that yourself," Gretchen pointed out. "So you shouldn't complain."

I couldn't believe she was being so callous. What were friends *for*, if not to complain to? "You want to trade? You take my place at Woodson and we'll see how long you last. We'll see how *you* like putting up with vindictive teachers and millions of hateful kids!"

"Poor little Kobie."

I was ready to hang up on her. "Some best friend *you* are, Gretchen Farris! Where are you when I need you?"

"And where are *you* when I need you?" Gretchen returned. "You don't need me for a best friend, Kobie. You've already got one — yourself."

"What's *that* supposed to mean?"

"You're so smart, you figure it out." And she hung up on me before I could hang up on her.

Chapter 10

My mother did not murder me over my bad report card. I wish she had. Because then I wouldn't have started a Slam Book, which, as it turned out, spelled the beginning of the end for me.

Instead of stringing me up in the backyard or having me shot at dawn, as I expected her to do, my mother opted for that age-old mothers' method of torture, the Endless Lecture. From the instant her eyes lit on the F in home ec, my mother lingered over that failing grade, almost ignoring my A's and Miss Channing's request for a conference.

Her voice followed me everywhere, in the bathroom, in my room, at the supper table, even in the car. I was unable to escape it. Her lecture poured out of the speakers of my record player, drifted out from under my bed, trailed up from the pages of magazines, and leaked out of the toothpaste tube, until I regretted the day I was born and then the day *she* was born.

I was worn down to a nubbin at home and agitated to a frazzle at school. Then Thanksgiving vacation arrived, bringing me relief from the strife of Woodson. My mother got busy with the festivities and let up her lecturing. She didn't even mention the conference with Miss Channing. Her silence was so marked and profound, I thought I had gone deaf.

I couldn't even visit Gretchen, as I usually did on long weekends. She was in Frederick, Maryland, staying a few days with her cousin. Not that we were getting along all that well. Ever since report card day, things had been icy between us. We still sat next to each other on the bus and we talked on the phone, but it wasn't the same. Gretchen acted indifferent, as if she didn't care whether I sat next to her or called her up or dropped off the face of the earth. I was beginning to wonder if our lease as best friends had run out and nobody had informed me. I had the feeling that if we were up for renewal for another eight-year term as best friends, Gretchen wouldn't sign on the dotted line.

It was during Thanksgiving vacation that I quit moping around long enough to start a Slam Book, and, coincidentally, draw up my own death certificate.

Marianne Andrews revived the tradition of Slam Books at Woodson. She came to geography class one day and, instead of snipping her split ends and gossiping with her friend Barbara Phillips, she took out a new spiral notebook and wrote in it the whole period. When class was over, Mr. Eaton, evidently thinking his pet had actually done a little class work, praised her to the stars for her diligence.

The next day, Marianne handed the notebook to Barbara. I shamelessly listened to their conversation, while Mr. Eaton droned on about the imports of Lithuania.

"What's this?" Barbara asked.

"It's a Slam Book," Marianne replied. "You know my sister who's in college? Well, she told me about them. They were all the rage when she was in high school, so I thought I'd start one."

Barbara flipped through the notebook. "What do you do with it?"

"Answer the question," Marianne said. "But don't sign your name. It's supposed to be anonymous. The idea is to get a whole bunch of them going at once, so nobody knows who's Slam Book they've got."

I had heard enough about Slam Books, intermixed with textiles and sheep farming, to be filled with curiosity by the time Barbara passed Marianne's Slam Book to the girl next to me. When the Slam Book crossed my desk, en route back to Marianne, I sneaked a peek inside.

Each page had one question written at the top. The questions began fairly innocently — *What's your favorite color, song, TV show* — progressing to meatier issues, such as *Who do you think is the cutest guy in the school?* Then there were pages and pages of just names, and this was where the "slamming" began. Apparently, you were supposed to write exactly what you thought of a particular person, no holding back. Since there were no signatures involved, you couldn't tell who wrote what about whom. On one page was Marianne's own name, but the comments, from my cursory glance, seemed pretty safe: "Prettiest girl in Woodson," "Great hair," "Good dancer," etc.

I looked up at Marianne as I was about to hand her Slam Book to Eddie Showalter. She must have seen me peeking in her Slam Book. She gave me a tiny smile. For one mind-reeling instant, I thought Marianne was signaling me permission to sign her Slam Book, sort of an initiation ceremony into her special group. But then she frowned, and I realized she wanted me to pass her book over.

Within days, Slam Books were the latest craze among the freshman class. Everyplace I went, I saw girls swapping spiral notebooks. In math and French, I enviously watched friends writing in one another's Slam Books. I longed to be part of that group, brave enough to start a fad, confident enough to hand my Slam Book to anyone and know that no one would write anything derogatory on the page headed with my own name.

The Saturday after Thanksgiving, I was sulking in my room, snuffling over the fact that nobody loved me, when I hit upon the notion of starting my own Slam Book. Initially, it was going to be a joke — a place I would vent my feelings by inscribing what I thought of all the people I envied at the moment.

But the idea of having my very own Slam Book to carry around Woodson festered and grew. I could flash my Slam Book in French class, pretend to read comments written by the vast hordes of my nonexistent friends, even chuckle at appropriate intervals. I was also tired of drawing and being by myself. The Slam Book project gave me something to do and took my mind off my troubles.

While I rooted through my junk for an unused spiral notebook, it never occurred to me that instituting a Slam Book would compound my troubles, zillionfold.

I lay on my stomach on my purple carpet, playing one of the two record albums I owned. With a new cartridge in my ink pen, I neatly printed silly, trivial questions: *What is your favorite color? Who is your favorite rock singer?* I quickly ran out of names on the "name" pages, though, since I only had one person I could call a friend and her status was up in the air at the moment. Throwing all caution to the wind — because, after all, who would see this notebook? — I scribbled the names of Sandy Robertson, Marianne Andrews, Jeanette Adams, Barbara Phillips, Cheryl Ramsey, Stuart Buckley, and Eddie Showalter. At the end, I wrote my own name. Seeing "Kobie Roberts" meticulously printed in my own handwriting filled me with a sense of sadness. The Slam Book exercise only served to point up how far outside Marianne's circle I really was.

On Monday I gave my Slam Book to Gretchen, as a kind of peace offering.

"Oh, you've got those at Woodson, too," she said, in the bored tone of someone who'd been pressed to sign Slam Books day and night for weeks. As the bus jolted over the highway, she answered the questions at the front of my book. When she got to the "name" pages at the back, she put her pen away. "Kobie, I don't know any of these people, except Stuart."

I didn't know them either, I started to say. Instead I took my Slam Book back from her, peeved she hadn't at least turned to the page with my name on it. I guess I would never learn what Gretchen thought of me these days.

I meant to leave my Slam Book in my locker but foolishly changed my mind and stacked it conspicuously on top of my textbooks, so that other kids would see that I had a Slam Book, too.

At the head table in home ec, Miss Channing endeavored to make a milkshake in a blender.

Sandy spied my Slam Book. "Can I write in it?" she begged. "I haven't written in anybody's yet. Please, Kobie?"

"Sure, go ahead," I said carelessly, muffling a giggle as Miss Channing turned on the blender without securing the top. Vanilla milkshake spewed all over the place.

Sandy bent earnestly over my Slam Book, deliberating over each question as if she were drafting the Magna Charta. She looked up at me once and said, "Boy, this is fun. I'm going to start a Slam Book, and you can be the first to write in it."

I was sorry I had let Sandy see my Slam Book. It wasn't good for unpopular people like us to have a taste of being in the in crowd. First, circle pins, then Slam Books; who knew what we'd crave next? We might even lose control and do something nervy and presumptuous, like try to sit with Marianne's group at lunch. When Marianne slapped us back down into the unpopular pit, it was going to hurt.

After making a mess of staggering proportions, Miss Channing blithely invited the class back to the test kitchen to watch her whip up another little treat in her trusty blender.

When the bell rang, we ran back to our table to gather our things.

"Here's your Slam Book," Sandy said. "I'll finish it tomorrow, if that's okay."

I sauntered into geography class, parading by Marianne's desk with my Slam Book prominently displayed. Naturally, she wasn't paying any attention. But Eddie Showalter was. He looked up from shading the west wing of the White House he had drawn on his desktop.

"I see you've got one, too," he said, referring to my Slam Book. "Do girls really write about boys in those books?"

"I just started mine," I told him. "You can look in it if you want."

Eddie eagerly leafed through my Slam Book. Boys weren't allowed to see the books, mainly because girls were antsy at the prospect of the boys finding out what was thought about them. I remembered with a stab of panic that I had included Eddie in the "name" pages. If Eddie saw his name, he might get the wrong idea.

"Mr. Eaton's coming," I hissed. "Quick, give it back."

"It's kind of dumb," Eddie declared. "All that junk about rock stars. But whoever wrote that about Jeanette Adams better watch out. She wrote something really nasty."

I ripped through the notebook until I came to the page headed "Jeanette Adams." In her up-and-down handwriting, Sandy had scrawled, "Dumb bleached blonde who couldn't get a boyfriend if she walked down the street in a bikini!"

My throat constricted in horror. Sandy had actually written that about Jeanette "Killer" Adams in my book! How stupid could she get? You *didn't* "slam" Jeanette Adams! Thank heavens Jeanette had skipped home ec today. Suppose Sandy had left my book open to that page when we went back to the test kitchen and Jeanette had somehow seen it?

But Jeanette *had* skipped home ec, and no one except Eddie had seen this page. I tore it out of the spiral notebook with a sudden zipping sound that caused Mr. Eaton to pause in his rambles about the annual rainfall in Albania. I ripped the page in half and the halves into quarters and eighths and sixteenths. When the pieces were small enough, I considered chewing them up, just to make sure that Jeanette would never see what Sandy had written.

I compromised by throwing the scraps in Mr. Eaton's trash can, then grilled him about the trash pickup.

"Are you *sure* the wastebaskets are emptied every single day and the trash is burned in the incinerator?" I quizzed. In this matter, I couldn't afford to be too cautious. And I knew I wouldn't sleep a wink until I was certain that Sandy's comment was in ashes at the bottom of the big Dumpster and the Dumpster was on its way to the county landfill.

But even if I had personally supervised the burning of the day's trash and buried the ashes in my backyard by the light of the moon, it wouldn't have done any good, I soon learned.

Later that same day, as Sandy and I were changing into our gymsuits, I felt a vise clamp my upper arm. Slowly, the vise twisted me until I was nose to nose with Jeanette Adams. A thick, liquid fear like Miss Channing's milkshake rippled down my backbone.

"I saw what you wrote about me in that

book," Jeanette said menacingly. "Couldn't get a boyfriend even if I walked down the street in a bikini, huh?"

My worst nightmare had come true! Jeanette must have slipped into home ec long enough to see what Sandy had written about her and then immediately went to arrange my funeral.

"What book?" She was holding me almost off the floor, and my voice came out in a high-pitched squeak. Beside me, Sandy was goggle-eyed.

"*You* know what book. Now I'm going to make you sorry you wrote it," Jeanette snarled.

I was already sorry, and I hadn't written *any*thing. If I wanted to live to see the sun rise tomorrow, I had better clear up this little misunderstanding and fast. I laughed, but it sounded more like a whinny. "Jeanette, that was my book you saw, but I didn't write that remark. Hah-hah!"

"Who did?" Jeanette demanded.

Sandy was trying to slither away. Much as I wanted to deflect Jeanette's fury to the right party, I couldn't snitch on anybody who wore orthopedic shoes. "I don't know," I stammered. "I gave my Slam Book to lots of people today. You know how it works — nobody signs their name."

Jeanette tightened her grip. The circulation in my arm stopped just below her tourniquetlike fingers. "Whose Slam Book was it?"

"Kobie's!" Sandy yelled.

"Sandy's!" I cried simultaneously. Jeanette had me so rattled, I didn't know what I was saying. "It was Slandy's Sam Book! I mean, Sandy's Slam Book. We don't know who wrote in it, do we, Sandy?" I aimed a desperate look in her direction.

"It could have been anybody. At least fifty people signed it," Sandy fibbed.

Jeanette curled her lip. "Then how come I only saw two kinds of handwriting? And only *one* handwriting on my page." Her face was very close to mine. "Yours."

"It wasn't mine," I said weakly.

"Yes, it was," Jeanette insisted. "Only you would call me a dumb bleached blonde." She shoved me up against the locker, her smile a terrible thing to behold. "I wouldn't give two cents for your life right now."

I rubbed my arm. In view of the circumstances, I thought her offer was really quite generous.

Chapter 11

My mother often told me I was my own worst enemy. Maybe so, but I couldn't hold a candle to Jeanette Adams. Jeanette was a master at making my life wretched.

After the Slam Book incident, she started coming regularly to home ec, just to bug me. She would sit across from me at the table and clean her nails, a threatening presence. Other times she would move so she was sitting right next to me, her chair too close to mine for comfort. Occasionally, after one of Miss Channing's demonstrations in the test kitchen, I would come back to our table and find scribbles all over my notes. And once someone, presumably Jeanette, tore up my geography homework. She never *said* anything to me, but I knew she was goading me, daring me into a confrontation.

"Just ignore her," Sandy would whisper.

Sandy, whose smart-aleck comment in my Slam Book started this whole affair, convinced me to go see Mr. Richards.

"He's no help," I told her, disheartened. "Sure, Mr. Richards talks a good game, but he won't take any action. Nobody in this school ever does anything."

"It can't hurt," Sandy insisted, and dragged me into the guidance counselor's office.

Mr. Richards listened intently to my story, but when I finished, he took the old grown-up's cop-out I predicted he would.

"Kobie, you don't have any real proof that Jeanette did those things — ripped your paper and all. You *think* she did it. I can't bring her down to the office for that. And as for the other things — well, it's hardly a crime to sit next to someone in class or look at someone across the table." His attitude softened a bit. "I understand you're having problems, but — "

"You *don't* understand!" I fired back. "You're not there, so you can't understand!" I left his office, frustrated and angry. Was there no one I could go to about Jeanette?

Certainly not my best friend. Gretchen was mad at me, and I didn't even know why. On the bus, she gazed out the window, responding to me in monosyllables. Whenever I'd call her on the phone, she always claimed she was busy, that she had homework and couldn't talk. With our conversations reduced to shorthand, it was impossible to confide in her.

I considered, for about one twelfth of a second, asking my mother for advice, but if I so much as mentioned a problem in home ec, she'd be off about the F I got in that class. According to my mother, everything was my fault. I got an F simply because I "wasn't paying attention." That was the only reason Miss Channing gave me a failing grade. I'd like to see how attentive *she'd* be in class, with Jack the Ripper waving a sharp nail file under her nose.

Stuart Buckley was waiting by my locker one frosty December morning, his hands jammed into his jacket pockets. He looked as forlorn as I felt. I remembered the last day of eighth grade when Stuart and I had shaken hands and wished each other good luck at Woodson. Some luck we were having! Both of us persecuted by a couple of bullies!

"Are you still paying that guy off?" I asked him.

"Yeah. Want to donate to the needy?"

Stuart appeared to have lost his bounce — the boy that was picking on him was clearly winning.

"Stuart, you really ought to tell somebody about this," I said, fishing three dimes out of my purse. "This guy knows he's got a good thing going, hitting on a freshman."

"Who would I go see?" Stuart said, more as a challenge than a question. "Who's going to believe the word of a little guy like me against a big tough senior? The minute I open my mouth, that guy will be all over me like a wet sheet."

He was right. Freshmen were at the bottom of the totem pole — we had practically no voice in this school, not that anyone was around to hear us even if we did. I wondered if I could pay off Jeanette, the way Stuart was paying that big senior boy to leave him alone. But Stuart hadn't really done anything to the senior, except show up in school and look like an easy mark. But my case was different. Jeanette was riled. As long as she thought I wrote that ridiculous comment in my Slam Book, no amount of money could appease her. Jeanette was out for blood.

"Hey, Kobie, I got a surprise for you," my father announced, coming home from work early one evening.

He had been putting in a lot of overtime

lately and for a good reason. I'd heard my parents talking about how the property taxes had doubled that year. Real estate taxes were due in two installments, the first part in July, around my birthday, and the second half in December. I often wondered who thought up that schedule, to make people pay out a huge sum of money before Christmas and their only child's birthday. But at least I knew why my mother was so preoccupied.

"A surprise for me? What is it?" Maybe Dad had bought me a one-way ticket to Pago Pago.

"Come out to the truck and see."

Mom and I went outside. Dad had driven home the county pickup he used for work. In the back, anchored by ropes, was some sort of filing cabinet.

"Is that mine?" I asked dubiously. Presents come in all shapes and sizes, and normally I wasn't too choosy, but this one didn't look like much.

My father unlatched the tailgate. "It's a parts cabinet. We're getting a new one in the shop, and they let me have the old one. I thought you could use it for your drawings."

A parts cabinet for my drawings? The dun-colored enamel was chipped and scratched. The drawers were shallow, designed to hold small parts, and divided into little cubbyholes. I didn't want to hurt my father's feelings, but I couldn't see how I could get my oversize drawings into the cabinet.

My mother examined the cabinet once it was off the truck. "Look, Kobie," she said. "These dividers slip right out. You can lay your drawings in flat and they won't get wrinkled. Or you can leave the dividers in one drawer for your art supplies. And we can paint it any color you want."

Now I could see the possibilities. It *was* a perfect present. I hugged my father. Then Mom and I went to the store to buy a can of spray paint. I chose a bright, cheery turquoise. Mom helped me spray my cabinet and polish the brass hardware until the fittings gleamed like gold. Using lime-green construction paper, I cut out inserts to label the drawers.

Against my new royal purple carpet, the turquoise cabinet made an imposing sight. For the first time since I had decided to become an animator, I felt like I was truly on my way — my room seemed less like a bedroom and more like a serious working place. I spent the weekend sifting through my drawings and filing them in my cabinet by category.

"Kobie!" my mother exclaimed. "Your room! I can't believe it."

I stowed a bundle of sketches in the drawer labeled "Cinderella" — last year's art project — and slid the drawer shut, enjoying the businesslike click of the rollers. "Doesn't look too bad, does it? I never realized how much of the mess had been drawings." My room *did* look a lot better now that it was straight, but I'd rather be staked to an anthill than admit as much to my mother.

"Now if you'd just pick up your clothes — " she began.

"Let's not go overboard," I said, borrowing one of her expressions.

I thought she'd yell at me for being fresh, but she just smiled and sat down on my lumpy bed. "You've been kind of quiet lately. How come you never talk about Gretchen anymore? Are the two of you on the outs?"

"One of us is." I twirled a protractor on the end of my index finger. "She's mad at me and I have no idea why."

"Did you say something to hurt her feelings?"

"No! Nothing! I don't know what her major malfunction is." I fiddled with a scrap of lime-green paper. My mother and I were actually talking, not arguing. It felt funny. I imagined this was how soldiers felt during the Christmas truce, trading jokes across the trenches, knowing they'd soon be shooting at one another again.

"It must be rough for Gretchen, repeating a grade," Mom said. I wanted to tell her it wasn't any trip to the beach for me, either, but she went on. "I saw her mother in the A&P the other day. She said Gretchen is trying so hard to catch up, she studies all the time. Gretchen has problems."

"Who doesn't?" She was starting to sound like Mr. Richards.

"When you talk to Gretchen, do you ever ask her how things are going with her? Or do you just talk about yourself?"

"What makes you think I do that?"

"Well, Gretchen's at Frost again this year . . . you're in a new school — high school yet . . . it stands to reason that you'd talk mostly about what you're doing."

I mulled this over. "And you think Gretchen is mad at me because I haven't acted interested in what she's doing?"

My mother nodded, then added in her listen-to-me-I'm-older-and-wiser tone of voice, "You have to *be* a friend to have a friend. Life isn't a one-way street, Kobie."

If only I could boil all my troubles down to simple proverbs. I could see myself going up to Jeanette Adams and saying, "Let's bury the hatchet. Live and let live. Forgive and forget." Jeanette would probably retaliate with the maxim *she* lived by, "Drop dead."

I sighed. "Mom, when will things get better?"

"When you're fifteen, Kobie," my mother promised, making one of those sweeping generalizations based purely on instinct that mothers were famous for. "Things won't be so hard after you turn fifteen."

"Are you just saying that to shut me up?" I asked. "Like that time ages ago when I was pestering you about where the sun went at night and you said if I'd be quiet and good, you'd look up the answer in this magic book? For *years* I believed you really had a magic book."

My mother pretended she didn't know what I was talking about. "What magic book? I never said any such thing."

"You did, too! You told me it had a green cover and an old Gypsy woman gave it to you. I used to *dream* about that book, and I was sure you kept it hidden in the strongbox with my birth certificate and the fire insurance policy." One of the hardest lessons in my fourteen years was realizing that no magic book with the answers existed, that my mother had made it up to tease me.

She laughed. "Oh, Kobie! You had such an imagination, and you always took everything to heart. I was sorry I mentioned that book, but once it was out, you wouldn't forget about it." She looked at me. "You still take everything to heart. That's why these years are so difficult."

"And when I'm fifteen, it'll be different?"

"Twelve, thirteen, fourteen — those were tough years for me, too," my mother admitted. "But after I turned fifteen, things seemed to settle down." I figured she was talking about body changes and all that other girl-stuff. "I stopped fighting the world and learned to live in it. You will, too. You'll see."

I wanted to believe her, but I didn't think I could hold on that long. My fifteenth birthday wasn't until the next summer.

Since my room was reasonably clean, I put on an old jacket and went outdoors. It was a bracing fall day, with a wind that stripped dead leaves off the oaks in our front yard and scattered them over the hillside. When I was little, I used to try to catch leaves. I would stand about midway down the hill and track the wind-tossed path of one leaf, then I would run around chasing the leaf, which invariably landed in a different spot. I'd play that game for hours, but I hardly ever caught any leaves.

Now I tilted my head back and watched the dizzy flight of a leaf weaving like the tail of a kite. Friends were a lot like catching leaves, I decided. Just when you thought you had them figured, knew where they were going to land, they changed course and you wound up empty-handed.

"I'll be glad when it gets really cold and we have class inside," I remarked to Sandy one afternoon as we came in from the hockey field. My idea of fun was not standing around in a bloomer-legged gymsuit, freezing to death. "Look at my legs! They're blue!"

Sandy handed me my towel. "After Christmas, we're starting modern dance. That'll be indoors. I heard somebody say they make the boys watch!"

"Yippie. I've always wanted to entertain a roomful of freshmen boys by leaping around in this charming outfit." I unbuttoned my gymsuit, shivering. Today a hot shower would feel good, and we actually had enough time to take one. When we came out of the shower, dripping and giggling, I spotted Jeanette lounging next to our locker.

"What do you suppose she's been up to?" I asked, instantly suspicious.

"She hasn't taken our clothes in a long time. Maybe she just wants to talk," Sandy suggested.

My worst fears were confirmed — our

clothes were not in the locker. "Where did you put them?" I shrieked to Jeanette.

Her laughter was taunting.

Clutching our towels, Sandy and I scurried around the locker room, opening and slamming locker doors. The other girls were dressed and gone, except for a few calmly combing their hair in front of the mirrors.

Cheryl Ramsey watched me ransack the towel room. "What's with you guys?"

"Don't ask!"

We checked every single locker and thoroughly investigated the towel and shower rooms, short of prying up the drains, but we did not find our clothes.

"We may have to go home in these towels," Sandy said glumly.

I was bordering on hysterics. "She hid every stitch! Even our underwear! It's un-American to hide somebody's underwear! How mean can you *get*?"

Ms. Birmingham was putting away hockey equipment on the other side of the gym, so she was unaware of the crisis in the locker room.

"Jeanette, where are our clothes?" I screamed. The bell was about to ring. I didn't relish the notion of sleeping on a hard locker-room bench, covered with a damp towel.

"What makes you think I know anything about your clothes?" Jeanette said sweetly. "Terribly careless of you, Kobie, losing your clothes like that."

While I contemplated taking a crowbar to the floorboards, Sandy pawed through the trash cans.

"Here's your blouse!" she cried triumphantly just as the bell rang. "And my skirt!"

"Well, one of us can leave here, anyway," I said, snatching my blouse and putting it on.

"See you girls tomorrow!" Jeanette trilled. "Hope you don't get too chilly!"

Jeanette had outdone herself this time. She had buried our clothes in six different trash cans, under heaps of soggy paper towels. As a final inspiration, she had emptied the contents of our purses at the bottom of two waste bins.

Flinging paper towels all over the floor, Sandy and I grabbed our clothes and flung them on, fully aware that the bus drivers waited about 1.5 seconds after the bell before roaring out of the parking lot.

With my shoes on the wrong feet, my skirt unzipped, and my sweater on backward, I raced out to the loading zone. Sandy straggled behind me, unsuccessfully stuffing her billfold, lip gloss, keys, and about a thousand pieces of gum into her pocketbook as she ran.

"I've had it with that girl!" I declared, dropping my pantyhose and slip, which I hadn't had time to put on, in front of at least fifty sophomore boys. "This is the last straw!"

My bus was already revving up to pull out. I knuckled the closed door and pounded on the glass. The driver reluctantly let me in.

"I'm going to kill her!" I yelled.

Only someone half dressed, still wet, and temporarily deranged would utter such a foolhardy threat. Of course, no one but Sandy heard me. And how was I to know that Sandy would run and tell Jeanette first thing that I was gunning for her?

Chapter 12

"You told Jeanette *what*? For crying out loud, Sandy! Did you help her pick out my tombstone, too?"

Sandy was defensive. "I didn't mean to get you in trouble. I thought if I told Jeanette you were after her, she'd back off."

"When did Attila the Hun ever back off?" I demanded. "Honestly, Sandy."

Sandy had met me at the door of home-room with this jolly news. Hardly one to be quaking in her boots, Jeanette told Sandy to tell *me* that she'd be waiting for me in home ec. "With her bayonet," I groaned.

When Mrs. Benson called my name in the rollbook, I snapped, "Here!" And before she could finish saying Sandy's name, I cut in with, "She's here, too, but I wish she weren't." Mrs. Benson glanced up sharply, but went on taking attendance.

"I can't believe you did this to me," I said to Sandy. "I thought you were my *friend*." Well, that wasn't entirely true. I knew that *Sandy* thought we were friends, but I never really counted Sandy as a friend. She was a necessary evil, something I had to put up with, like a cold sore. Faced with a life span now shortened to about two hours, I stretched the truth to make my point.

Sandy seemed contrite. "I *am* your friend, Kobie. That's why I told Jeanette you were going to kill her. I was only trying to help."

"Help? With friends like you who needs enemies? Now Jeanette thinks I'm going to bump her off." I turned around in my seat and refused to speak to Sandy the rest of homeroom, no matter how many times she jabbed me in the back with her pencil.

Stuart was hanging around my locker between first and second periods. He held out his hand when he saw me coming. "Hiya, Kobie. What's new?"

I slapped his hand away. "Why don't you go beg on another corner, Stuart? This is getting old."

"What's with *you*? Did you get up on the wrong side of the bed?"

"None of your business."

Stuart actually looked hurt. "How come you smacked me?"

"Because I'm tired of your panhandling." I dug out my geography book.

"You think I only came by because I needed money?" he asked, as if terribly offended.

"That's the only time I see you." I decided to give him a fair chance. "All right. Why *are* you lurking around my locker if you don't want money?"

"I just wanted to say hi. Hi." Stuart wasn't very convincing, and he tried to cover it up by acting huffy. "If you're going to get snippy over lending a friend a little money, then I'll pay you back the three dollars I owe you."

"It's four-twenty-five. And pay me soon —I need it for Christmas," I said. "When are you going to pay me?"

Stuart was already sidling down the hall. "I don't know. Soon."

"I bet." Then I remembered an old phrase my mother used. "You know what you are, Stuart? A fair-weather friend. You only come around when you want something."

"Well, you're no kind of a friend at all!" he returned.

I wondered if he had gotten his quota to keep that big senior boy from using him as a whipping post another week. But then I dismissed Stuart's problem from my mind — I had worries of my own to deal with.

I crossed my fingers as I entered home ec, hoping against hope that Jeanette would be absent. But there she was at our table. My heart skittered at the sight of her.

Sandy ran in behind me. "Oh, Kobie! I thought I'd gotten here too late."

"Too late for what? Is she going to kill me right here in class? Miss Channing would probably love it." I felt trapped. I wished I had the nerve to skip class, but the teacher had already seen me. I had no choice, not the way Miss Channing dished out F's. I sat down as far away from Jeanette as I possibly could and still be in the same room.

Jeanette was fiddling with her nail file. "Hello, Kobie. Did you make the bus yesterday?"

"It wasn't funny, Jeanette. Sandy and I just barely made it. And I've told you a hundred times — I didn't write that remark in my Slam Book."

"But you *did* tell Sandy that you were going to kill me."

I said nothing. Even if I lied, Jeanette wouldn't buy it. She had it in for me and wasn't going to be happy until my mangled and bleeding body was lying at her size ten feet.

Jeanette ran her file under the edge of her inch-long fingernail. "I'll meet you in the back parking lot at lunch. And we'll just see who kills who." She said this mildly, as if she were ordering a pizza.

"It's whom," I said automatically. "Who kills whom." That was a barometer of my desperation, to correct the grammar of the thug who was scheduling my own murder.

Jeanette's eyes were hard as glass. "Who kills *whom*," she sneered. "I can't believe you, Kobie. You're going to die and you still have to get an A!"

"Listen, Jeanette," Sandy said. "Why don't we all go someplace and talk? If we get everything out in the open, I think we can — "

"Shut up," Jeanette ordered. "This is between Kobie and me."

And the funeral director, I thought with a sinking stomach. But it occurred to me that Jeanette was on the mark this time. Sandy was an annoying factor in our feud, like a fly buzzing around a wrestling match. Sparks had flared between me and Jeanette from the very first day of school, when Jeanette plunked herself down at our table and established herself as queen bee. She didn't like it that I got good grades in my non-Jeanette classes, and she was always taking potshots at me. Maybe because she thought I thought I was better than she was. Now she was bent on proving that brains didn't count, not in her world where things were settled in back parking lots.

"What's your lunch shift?" she asked me.

I looked at Sandy. This was *it*. I was actually setting a time for my demise.

"A — " Sandy blurted.

"D," I said at the same time. I hoped to throw Jeanette off the scent by telling her my *real* lunch shift, kind of reverse psychology. But then Blabberlips butt in and ruined things, as usual.

"Which is it?" Jeanette said. "A or D?"

I spoke first. "A — "

"D," Sandy put in.

"D, huh?" Jeanette chuckled. I had tried to foil her, but she wasn't stupid. Unlike some people I knew. I glared at Sandy, who gave me an apologetic shrug.

"I'll meet you Monday in the lot behind the Quonset huts," Jeanette commanded. "D lunch shift. You'd better show up. Because if you don't — " She drew the nail file across her own throat.

"Why Monday?" I asked inanely. "Why not today? Get it over with?"

Jeanette packed up her pocketbook. "Because I've got something better to do today during lunch."

"I guess it's tough finding space in your

appointment calendar to beat people up."
I could talk to Jeanette any old way now —
I had nothing to lose.

"You know," Jeanette said, "I'm really
looking forward to Monday." She walked
out in the middle of class, while Miss Channing was writing on the blackboard.

When she had gone, Sandy said, "She's
just bluffing, Kobie. Nothing's going to
happen Monday. She'll probably forget all
about it over the weekend."

I doubted it. Jeanette was not the type
to overlook the tiniest slight, much less that
stupid comment about her ability to get a
boyfriend. My fate was sealed.

In geography, Mr. Eaton popped a quiz
on us. In the middle of answering the questions, I ran out of ink. I always carried a
spare cartridge in my purse, but today I
couldn't seem to insert the cartridge properly. I poked a hole in one end of the plastic
cylinder with the point of my compass. Ink
dribbled out of the cartridge before I could
get it back in the pen. I wanted to cry. My
quiz paper was smudged with blue stains,
my pen was out of ink, and my life — what
was left of it — was in shambles.

Eddie Showalter reached across the aisle
and took my pen. Wordlessly, he inserted
the new cartridge, wiped the nib with his
handkerchief, then passed my pen back to

me. When the quiz was over, Mr. Eaton collected the papers, and let us talk the rest of the period.

"Thanks," I told Eddie. "I probably would have flunked if you hadn't come to my rescue." Then I thought of the futility of worrying over one geography quiz, when my life was going to end in less than three days.

"Don't mention it," Eddie said. "You don't look too good. Did you cook in home ec again today?"

I shook my head. "I — it's something else."

"Want to talk about it?" He really seemed interested in my troubles.

Eddie Showalter looked the same as always, wiggly eyebrows, beige sweater, one hand compulsively sketching the White House on the back of his notebook. His presence was comforting somehow. Eddie had sat next to me in geography class every day since school had started — he never changed. After Monday, I wondered if he would go on drawing and wearing his beige sweater, while the desk next to his remained pathetically empty, like Tiny Tim's crutch and stool by the fire. The world would go on, whether I was in it or not. The thought was so depressing I couldn't even answer Eddie.

* * *

Back when I was young and stupid, I often played a game with myself on nights I couldn't fall asleep right away. I'd pretend that some mysterious benefactor had given me a thousand dollars, but I had to spend it all that same day. I'd lie on my back and stare at the lights swishing across the ceiling from passing cars and plan what I'd buy with the money. When you're just a kid, it's hard to think of enough lavish purchases to use up a thousand dollars. I pictured myself going to the toy store first, and grandly buying the biggest and most elaborate chemistry set. And then on to the art supply store, where I'd buy all kinds of expensive pens and watercolors. I'd wind up at the grocery store and pile twenty carts with Twinkies and candy bars and cases of cream soda.

But before I could eat a single Twinkie or mix a test tube of vile-smelling chemicals, my daydream fizzled. I never came near spending that much money, even in my mind. The point is, it's tough to do anything that important in just one day. So imagine how tough it was to decide how to spend my last weekend on earth.

Friday evening I ate my solitary supper, scarcely tasting the corned beef hash and canned peas, racking my brain for some significant way to occupy my last two days. Maybe I would draw cartoons all weekend so that my parents would have enough sketches to hold a posthumous art show: "A Kobie Roberts Retrospective." Or maybe I would go around Saturday and Sunday doing good works so people would remember me as a kind, thoughtful person who cared about her fellow person.

I wound up reading comic books practically the whole time and playing scenes from my own funeral in my head. The line of people coming to pay their respects would wrap around the church and down the street. "Cut down in her prime," my friends would sob.

The scenario stopped right there. What friends? Who would mourn my passing? Not Gretchen. She hardly spoke to me these days. Certainly not Sandy Robertson. She'd probably tip my lifeless body out of the casket by mistake. "Oops!" she'd say. "Sorry, Kobie. I didn't mean it."

On Sunday, my parents went to Manassas to visit my mother's sister. Because they were only a few miles away, my mother let me stay home. Off they went, leaving their only daughter alone in her final hours. I watched them coast down the driveway until the car was out of sight. Then I went to call Gretchen.

I hated the idea of departing this world and not having anybody like me well enough to come to my memorial service.

Gretchen deserved an opportunity to make up to me — she'd probably regret it the rest of her life if I croaked while we were mad at each other.

She answered the phone anxiously.

"It's me," I said. "How are you doing?" Was I cool? On Death Row and I was asking my best friend how *she* was doing, just as my mother told me to. Kind, concerned, that's me.

"Oh, hi, Kobie." The enthusiasm drained noticeably from Gretchen's voice. "I can't really talk right now. I'm studying for a big test in science tomorrow. Did you want anything in particular?"

Did I want anything? Just to hear a friendly voice.

"No," I lied. "I just wondered how you were doing. That's all." I hung up and sat there by the silent telephone.

The coat closet was partly open, revealing a glimpse of wrapping paper. Christmas presents. The coat closet was my mother's not-very-original hiding place. Christmas was two whole weeks away. I wouldn't be here when my parents bought the tree from the JayCee lot in Centreville and decorated it. I wouldn't be here on Christmas morning to open all those wonderful-looking packages under the tree.

I decided to open them now.

I found three presents labeled "to Kobie."

Long ago I had learned the knack of sneaking into presents without tearing the wrapping. I eased the paper off the first box without even wrinkling it. Underwear! Not days-of-the-week underwear, as I had once sourly predicted to Gretchen, but nearly as bad. If all the presents were going to be that awful, maybe I shouldn't make myself feel worse by opening any more.

The next box intrigued me with its solid squareness, and I forgot about the disappointment of the underwear as I slid off the ribbon and paper. An electric razor, just for women! Was that mine? I checked the tag. It said "To Kobie, from Dad." My father was giving me an electric razor! I considered trying it out on my legs, but then realized my parents could get their money refunded if the razor was left unused in its box.

The smallest box was the hardest to sneak open. I ripped one corner of the paper in the process. A little Scotch tape would fix that up, though. I lifted the lid and gasped. Nestled in white cotton was a circle pin. Not a cheap one, like Sandy's, but real gold. The pin glimmered in the hall light.

The pin was so beautiful, I began to cry great big crocodile tears of self-pity. At first I was crying because I had spoiled

Christmas morning by peeking at my presents. Then I cried because my mother had finally broken down and gotten me one of the items on my right things list, and I wouldn't live to wear it!

Chapter 13

"I'm sick," I informed my mother Monday morning. "I can't go to school today."

My mother laid her cheek against my forehead, her way of determining my temperature. "You're not hot." She examined my face in a strong light to see if any disease had attacked me overnight. "Where are you sick?"

"All over. I just feel awful." The understatement of the decade. After sleeping in ten-second stints, I woke up this morning with such a feeling of doom hanging over me, I could hardly open my eyes.

"You look all right to me," said my mother. "Go on to school. If you feel worse by lunchtime, call me."

Undoubtedly I *would* be feeling much worse by lunchtime since I'd be dead along about then.

She handed me lunch money I would

never spend. "See you this afternoon."

"No, you won't," I replied bitterly and ran out of the house before she asked me to explain that cryptic remark.

All weekend I agonized over whether to tell my mother about Jeanette's threat. But my mother never seemed to light in one place long enough for me to get her attention. The best moment for a heavy discussion, like the upcoming demise of her only daughter, passed and I went to bed without saying good-night. I don't think she noticed. She won't even miss me when I don't get off the bus this afternoon. She might remember my existence sometime next week, when she goes to wash sheets.

Gretchen was in the last seat on the bus, reading her earth science book. There wasn't room to sit next to her, but I shoved myself in there anyway. I was hoping she'd comment on the dark circles under my eyes and ask me what was wrong, but she never looked up from her book. Between Gretchen and my mother, I was beginning to think that Jeanette was doing the world a favor by bumping me off.

I cleared my throat, not very subtly. "Still cramming for that test?"

"Yeah. Geology — I just can't seem to remember it." Our conversation was so impersonal, we might have been discussing the weather.

"Some of the stuff they make us learn is so dumb," I said. "Like rocks. If you've seen one rock, you've seen them all." Thinking about rocks led me to think about dirt and then about graves with big piles of dirt next to them. "My mother saw your mother in the grocery store the other day. Your mom said you've really been hitting the books lately."

Gretchen nodded. "It's hard taking two years in one. I never realized it would be so much work."

She went back to her studying and I stared out the window, realizing this was my last bus ride down Lee Highway. The last time I'd see Weber Tire Company, the last time I'd see Mister Donut, the last time I'd see Everly Funeral Home. . . .

I choked, fighting to keep from crying. I was scared and miserable and no one in the whole world cared a crumb. Not my best friend. Not even my own mother. The bus braked in front of Woodson. I gathered up my books and prepared to meet my fate.

"Kobie?" Gretchen called. I turned, my vision blurred with unshed tears. "Are you okay?" She looked as if she wanted to say more.

I shook my head numbly and stumbled

off the bus. Her concern came like an afterthought, too little, too late.

Sandy was pacing by our locker. "You're here! I didn't think you'd come to school today. You're so brave, Kobie."

"No, I'm not. I wanted to stay home like any sane coward, but I couldn't. My mother probably helped Jeanette set this up, so she could get rid of me."

"I saw Jeanette this morning. She wanted to know if you were here."

Maybe Jeanette had a change of heart and wanted to call the whole thing off. "How did she look? Remorseful?"

"Strong." Some morale-booster *she* was.

I died bit by bit in each of my classes as Eleventh Hour drew closer. I couldn't concentrate on anything but the clock, watching the hands advance relentlessly toward lunchtime.

When I didn't see Jeanette in home ec, a tiny bud of hope sprouted within me. Maybe she had finally been caught for skipping and was being detained in the office. But five minutes before the end of class, she appeared in the doorway. Imperiously, she motioned me to come to the door. I obeyed but stayed inside the room. As long as I didn't cross the invisible line, I felt some measure of protection.

"You showed," Jeanette said. "I thought you'd chicken out."

"My mother wouldn't let me."

"Too bad. I'll meet you in the back parking lot, D lunch. Be there or else."

I gulped, but the lump in my throat did not go away. Sandy was right: Jeanette *did* look strong today, raring to go. It wouldn't take her any time to polish off a puny little runt like me.

It reminded me of how I'd felt the time I'd climbed up the big water slide at Lake Fairfax. It had looked like such fun until I'd gotten to the top of the ladder and had seen jets of water sheeting the slide, water that whooshed kids to the bottom where they were dunked in deep water. I couldn't swim, but climbing down a ladderful of kids was impossible. There was no turning back — I had to go down that slide and suffer the consequences. If I didn't meet Jeanette in the parking lot during D lunch, I'd only be postponing the inevitable.

"She's going to do it," I told Sandy. "She's going to murder me, and I don't even get to eat lunch first."

"Go see Mr. Richards! He'll help you this time."

"Sandy, will you give up on that man? He's only a guidance counselor, not Superman. Besides, he always acts like we're interrupting something important." The bell rang, but I was unable to move, unable to head for geography, the class I had before lunch. I was scared witless. My face must have revealed my terror.

"We'll go right now," Sandy said, steering me by the arm. "Mr. Richards won't be too busy. He'll know what to do."

In the course of his career in advising students, I'm sure Mr. Richards had never heard a tale as wild as mine, especially since the storyteller was clearly irrational. And after every ludicrous claim I made, Sandy chorused, like a one-girl cheerleading section, "It's true!"

"Kobie," Mr. Richards said. "I can see you're frightened, but I think you're making too much of this."

"Making too much of my own *murder*!" I exclaimed.

"Do you really believe everything Jeanette Adams tells you?" he asked. "She talks about her mother, and Mrs. Adams doesn't live with the family. She brags about a boyfriend — what did you call him — a Viper? How do you know he exists? She probably wants to impress you girls and so she invented a tough boyfriend to enhance her image."

What difference did it make if Jeanette lied about her boyfriend? It was easy enough for Mr. Richards to sit there and theorize about Jeanette's love life — *he* wasn't going to die in forty minutes.

"Mr. Richards, you just don't understand this girl. She means *business*! If she says she's going to kill me, she's *going to kill me!*" Why couldn't I get through to him?

A secretary poked her head in the door. "Two students are waiting to see you, Mr. Richards. And there's that staff meeting in five minutes."

"Can't you call Jeanette down to the office and get her expelled?" Sandy said when the secretary was gone. Sandy looked almost as bad as I felt. I wanted to send *her* out to the parking lot in my place, since this whole mess was all her fault.

Mr. Richards smiled. "That's rather drastic, don't you think?"

"And dying isn't?"

The secretary popped in the doorway again and held up three fingers. Either there were three students waiting to see him or he had three minutes to get to that meeting. Despite what Sandy said, Mr. Richards was too busy to be bothered by a trivial matter like murder.

"All right, Kobie," he relented. "You go on back to class." He scribbled me a pass, in a rush to get to his meeting. "I'll arrange for Jeanette and you and me to get together and talk this over. I think we'll find that Jeanette has trouble making friends and this is her way of getting attention.

She just doesn't know how to show you she likes you."

That was the last straw. "Likes me! The girl wants to *kill* me!" I jumped to my feet, feverish with frustration. "I *knew* you'd let me down! Nobody in this dumb school ever does anything! I know a kid who has to pay off a big bully to keep him from beating him up. That stuff goes on all the time. Kids in this school get away with — murder! You'll be sorry you didn't help me, Mr. Richards. It'll be blood on your hands," I finished melodramatically and ran out of his office.

Behind me I could hear him calling me back and Sandy shrieking, "Kobie's going to die! Kobie's going to be killed!"

I pushed through the heavy front doors as if they were made of spun sugar and raced down the hill to the path that led to Robert Frost. I was sick of Mr. Richards and the whole school. Maybe the rest of them were content to twiddle their thumbs and let me be slaughtered, but I wasn't! It was time to take charge of my own life.

Woodson High and Robert Frost were separated by a wide field. I could see the back parking lot of Woodson, with its ocean of cars, but no sign of Jeanette. Tall weeds clawed my bare knees, and a stiff wind raked across the open space, but none of that mattered. Realizing I missed my old junior high terribly, I ran to Frost, where the routine was familiar and nobody wanted me dead. The sight of the halls filled me with nostalgia. If only I had been left back like Gretchen — none of this would be happening.

Mrs. Ryerson, my art teacher, had been very nice to me last year, praising my drawings and giving me a Rapidograph pen so I could keep up my art during the summer. I thought she would help me out of this jam. But once I was actually inside the school, I wondered just how helpful Mrs. Ryerson would be. She'd probably tell me to go back to class like Mr. Richards had.

I remembered that Gretchen had independent study during this time. Hoping no one would demand to see a pass, I scurried to the library. I found Gretchen at an empty table. The kids at other tables around her looked so *young.*

"Kobie! What on earth — ?"

"Gretchen, come out in the hall with me," I whispered.

When we were alone, I spilled my story. "I'm in so deep I don't know what to do."

"Kobie, this is terrible! Why didn't you *tell* me?"

"I guess I should have, before it got this far."

The librarian came out then and shot us a dirty look, as if she knew I didn't belong there. Seeing Gretchen's misery made me aware of that, too — I *didn't* belong at Frost anymore.

"I have to go," I told Gretchen. "I don't want to get you in trouble."

"What are you going to do? Kobie, I won't be able to stand it, sitting in class while you're out there. . . ." She didn't complete her sentence, and I was grateful. We hugged like people about to embark on a transatlantic voyage, and I left.

I jogged past Woodson, half expecting Mr. Richards and Sandy and Jeanette to come running after me. But no one saw me leave the school grounds. I walked west on Route 236, heading toward Centreville. Even if I'd had on the right shoes and a warm coat, which I didn't, I couldn't have walked home; it was too far. But walking was my only alternative. I certainly couldn't go back to Woodson.

I had never felt so lonely in my entire life. Cars sped past me going east and west. I envied the people in those cars, having someplace to go, while I trudged wearily down the long, winding road.

When I reached the intersection of Route 123, I knew I had hiked a couple of miles. I had no idea what time it was. The clock on the bank building hadn't been right since 1957. I was hungry and thirsty and my shoes had rubbed blisters on my heels. I wasn't cold anymore, though. Exercise, and the thought of Jeanette waiting malevolently for me like a black widow spider, warmed me up.

I turned left on Chain Bridge Road to the side street that bordered the county office buildings. The Massey Tower, the only semiskyscraper in Fairfax, loomed against the leaden clouds. I wondered if my parents had paid their taxes yet. Last year my father took me with him to the tax assessment office. I was disappointed that we only had to go to the second floor. I wondered if my parents would have a sad Christmas this year without me, or if they'd take back my presents and squander the money on a cruise to the Bahamas.

When I came to the police station, I knew that I had been heading here all along. The law ought to take care of Jeanette, if nobody at Woodson would. The blisters would be worth it to blow the whistle on Woodson, let people know what was *really* going on in the halls of learning.

The lobby of the police station bustled with officers clicking purposefully back and forth on the marbled floor in their shiny black shoes. Those shoes, more than the guns holstered to the men's belts, intimidated me. A police officer behind the counter barked, "Can I help you?"

I cringed and realized how foolish I was to come here. These were busy people with better things to do than waste their time on a stupid high school freshman.

"I — I'd like a drink of water. Can you tell me where the fountain is?"

The officer gave me a peculiar look, but directed me to the rest rooms down in the basement. I got my drink, then collapsed on the steps in the enclosed stairwell, exhausted. I was in serious trouble for leaving the school grounds. Nobody knew where I was. I was miles from home and miles from school. I couldn't move, couldn't think what to do next.

So I did what any self-respecting fourteen-year-old girl does when she's in trouble — I cried. I put my head down on my knees and let the tears flow.

A door slammed and the wandering, disembodied sound of humming floated above me. Feet pattered across the metal landing and down the steps. Before I could get up, a man in a brown suit stood over me.

"Something the matter, young lady?" he inquired. He seemed kind and fatherly, and that made me sob even harder.

"Are you hurt?" He bent down to touch my shoulder.

"Just my feet," I snuffled.

"What's wrong with your feet?"

"I walked all the way from Woodson."

"You walked from Woodson," he repeated. "I think you'd better come into my office."

"I can't. I don't know who you are."

He pulled his ID case from his pocket. "Lt. Rizzoli, Homicide."

And then I knew I had come to the right place after all. I stopped sniveling and said, "Just the person I want to see. I'd like to report an attempted murder."

Chapter 14

Lt. Rizzoli settled me in his office with a soft drink and a package of peanut butter crackers from the vending machines before asking, "Now, about this murder you wanted to report."

"Attempted murder," I corrected, my mouth full of crackers. I was starving.

"*Attempted* murder. Can you tell me who was about to be — done away with?" he finished delicately.

"I sure can. It was me." Washing down the dry crackers with an unladylike gulp of soda, I proceeded to relate my grisly tale.

When I was through, the lieutenant stared at me a few moments, as if trying to decide whether to bundle me in a basket and drop me on somebody else's doorstep or call in the man with the net.

"It's the truth," I said.

"Oh, I don't doubt it," Lt. Rizzoli said. "You must have been real scared to leave the school grounds the way you did." He leaned back in his chair and put his feet on his desk. "You know, when I was in the seventh grade, there was this kid who had it in for me. I got so I hated to go to school, because of that kid."

"What did you do?" Besides grow up and become a homicide detective, I nearly added.

"Nothing. He was bigger than me, and he had a lot of big mean friends."

Hardly a story to bolster my confidence in the local police force. "You didn't do *any*thing?" I asked, incredulous.

"Not that year. The *next* year I grew five inches, and for some reason that guy never bothered me again."

I swallowed the last of my soda. "And the moral is?"

Lt. Rizzoli swung his feet off his desk. "There is no moral, Kobie. You just do the best you can in this world. That's all you really can do."

I was hoping for something a little more substantial, like twenty-four-hour police protection or, at the very least, the pleasure of seeing Jeanette locked behind bars. After all, she threatened to *murder* me. Then I remembered I was in trouble myself, for running away from school.

"Are you going to send me to juvenile hall?" I asked.

The lieutenant was leafing through a county directory. "Nah. But I am going to have to send you back to school. You're still afraid of that girl, aren't you? You think she's going to kill you? Kobie, kids say stuff like that all the time. This girl knows you're scared; she's got you running — literally. She won't lay a hand on you."

"That's because she'll have to stand in line," I said darkly. "My mother will want first crack at me and then Mr. Richards and then the principal — "

"I'll take care of them." He reached for the phone. First he called Mr. Richards. I learned that my mother had been summoned and was in Mr. Richards' office right at that moment. I wondered how she felt making a hasty, unscheduled trip in the car. The lieutenant detailed my sordid afternoon and told Mr. Richards to go easy on me, that my feet hurt from my long walk. He hung up and dialed again, this time requesting a man named Bostic to drive me back to Woodson.

I stood up, brushing cracker crumbs from my skirt. "Well, thanks for the food. You've been very nice."

Lt. Rizzoli smiled. "I know it's rough going back, Kobie, but the school day isn't over, and technically, that's where you belong. Don't worry — everything will work out. Someday you'll look back on this as a big adventure."

Who said I'd live that long? He *was* sending me back to the lions' den. I tried to bargain for more time. "Listen, as long as I've missed this much school, what's another hour? How about letting me be your assistant? I can sharpen pencils and answer the phone, take out your empty coffee cups. . . ."

He laughed. "Maybe in a few years." We went outside. "If you're ever in the neighborhood again, drop in."

My driver, a brawny young police officer, was leaning against the fender of a squad car. A squad car! I was going back to school in *that*?

"Take this young lady to Woodson High School," Lt. Rizzoli ordered. "Don't just drop her off. Escort her to her guidance counselor's office." Why didn't he handcuff me if he was afraid I'd run away again? To me he said, "Chin up, Kobie. Things will be okay — you have my word."

The police officer put me in the backseat, behind the grille. The car smelled of old socks and the anxious sweat of desperate people like me. He didn't use blinking lights or the siren, but I still felt as if I was in a rerun of *Dragnet*.

174

It had taken me hours, it seemed, to walk from Woodson to the police station, but within minutes we were pulling up to the curb, ahead of the buses. The officer leaped nimbly from his side and came around to open my door. He even helped me out of the car. Suddenly I was transformed from a criminal to a movie star at a Hollywood premiere.

Flashbulbs didn't pop, but there were plenty of popping eyes as I made my entrance with the beefy-looking police officer. Everybody in the entire school was either hanging out the doors or running around the lobby. When they saw me and my bodyguard, they stopped dead in their tracks to gawk at us. The officer strode through the crowd, oblivious of the sensation he and I were creating.

Sandy and Stuart saw us and ran over.

"Kobie!" Sandy cried. "You're all right! I thought you met Jeanette and she killed you and stuffed your dead body under a car in the parking lot! I've been looking under cars all afternoon. Stuart helped."

My head was spinning. "Stuart helped stuff a dead body under the parking lot? Sandy, what are you talking about?"

"Never mind. You're here now." Impulsively, she threw her arms around me. "Kobie, I promise I won't get you in trouble ever again. I'll go after Jeanette myself."

"Maybe you won't have to," Stuart said. "Isn't that her over there?"

Sure enough, Jeanette was going into one of the vice-principal's offices. She stared at me and my escort, her eyes taking in the nightstick and pistol strapped to his belt.

"Is that the girl who's been giving you grief?" Officer Bostic asked. I nodded and he straightened up to eyeball Jeanette. One look from my burly cop was all it took. Jeanette went into the vice-principal's office. Had Lt. Rizzoli purposely picked the Incredible Hulk to bring me back to school, knowing Jeanette would see him and realize I had friends in high places? The lieutenant *did* promise that things would work out.

"I don't think she'll bother you anymore, Kobie," Stuart said. "Hey, can I borrow your police officer awhile? Maybe he'll scare off that big senior."

"Get your own police officer." What was the matter with Sandy and Stuart? They acted as if there was cause for celebration. Didn't they realize I was in serious trouble, to be sent back to school with a police officer?

In Mr. Richards' office, I found my mother twisting a tissue and moaning, "I don't know what I'm going to do with that girl!" When she saw the huge police officer bringing me in, she wailed, "See what I mean?"

"Mo-om!" I exclaimed. "You act like I'm delinquent every day of the week!"

Mr. Richards got up from behind his desk and thanked Officer Bostic, who left, undoubtedly relieved. He shut the door, but not before I saw the astonished faces of secretaries and other advisers. Even in a school as wild as Woodson, it wasn't exactly an everyday occurrence to see a police officer.

"Sit down, Kobie," Mr. Richards said. "You've had quite a day, haven't you?" I couldn't tell if he was mad or merely being polite in front of my mother. "It's been pretty exciting around here, too. Sandy and another boy disappeared. I finally located them in the parking lot, looking for you. The school's been in an uproar since you left, Kobie."

My mother sniffled.

"Mom, quit crying," I muttered in an undertone. "You're embarrassing me!"

"I'm embarrassing you!" she yelled, completely forgetting where she was. "I've been worried *sick* ever since Mr. Richards called me. What's the matter with you? Running off and getting everybody upset!" She might just as well have added, "The very idea! All this commotion simply because some girl threatened to murder you!"

"Your mother is right, Kobie," Mr. Richards said. "We *have* been worried. You know we're responsible for your welfare from the time that bell rings in the morning until you step off the bus in front of your house. What if something had happened to you?"

I couldn't believe what I was hearing. "Something *was* going to happen to me! Jeanette Adams wanted to beat me up! How come *I'm* the one being yelled at?"

"Because you were the one who left school property," Mr. Richards replied evenly.

"Yeah, but she *made* me — "

He held up his hand. "Nobody's yelling at you, Kobie. Your Lt. Rizzoli told me to go easy on you, which I intended to do — I just wanted you back where you belong, that's all. And I want to impress upon you the seriousness — the rashness — of your behavior."

"Nothing's going to happen to me?" I asked hopefully.

"You mean punitive action? No, nothing's going to happen."

I looked at my mother. "What about you? Lt. Rizzoli said *everybody* should go easy on me."

"I don't know about any police lieutenant. If I had my way. . . ." But then my mother said, "I'm partly to blame for this. You didn't feel you could confide in me. . . . I guess I've been too wrapped up in my own affairs lately. From now on I want to hear about what goes on at your school."

Boy, was she in for an earful. But I felt a little sorry for her, confessing she had shirked her motherly duties in front of my guidance counselor. I hadn't been the best daughter lately, either. Just like I hadn't been a good best friend.

Mr. Richards wasn't done with me yet. "Kobie, I know you think what you did was right, but it never pays to act on your own, not in this case. You should have trusted me. I want to help you — that's what I'm here for."

"You're always busy," I accused.

"Yes, we're all extra-busy this year, trying to handle the needs of four thousand students. It's not easy — and I'm not infallible. I'll try to do better next time . . . and so will you, right?"

"What's happening with Jeanette?" I asked. Time to fan the heat in her direction.

"Mr. Grafius called her in to question her about this incident and her skipping problem. I wouldn't want to be in Jeanette's shoes right now." Neither did I. Mr. Grafius was the toughest of all the vice-principals. "Your mother and I have had an interesting discussion while we were waiting for you to be brought back to school. In fact, she's having a conference today with your home ec teacher."

"Don't believe a word she says about me," I cautioned my mother. "That woman is — "

"Kobie!" my mother chided. "Don't be disrespectful!"

"Your mother told me you're very talented in art," Mr. Richards said. "And I said you have quite a reputation around here for being an escape artist. That's a joke, Kobie." He sighed when I didn't laugh. "Okay, I'll let you go. Stop by the office in the morning. I'll have a pass for the classes you missed today."

As he walked my mother to the door, I thought he gave her a conspiratorial wink. That was the trouble with parents and advisers getting together — they did all kinds of plotting and hatching behind a kid's back.

"I'm going to see Miss Channing," my mother said. "And then I'll drive you home, Kobie."

"What am I supposed to do while you're in with Miss Channing?"

"You can always talk to your friends," Mr. Richards said.

Friends? What friends? Except for Gretchen, who was my best friend now and always, I didn't have any friends. I thought about the goal I had set back in September, to have the right things so I would be accepted into the right group. My plan hadn't worked for Gretchen — she had all the right things, yet she was lonesome at Robert Frost.

Sandy and Stuart were waiting outside the main office. These were my friends? Sandy Robertson, who made solitude seem very desirable, and Stuart Buckley, who owed me money!

"Jeanette's still in there," Sandy said, pointing to Mr. Grafius's closed door. "Another vice-principal is in there with her. I wonder what they're doing to her."

"Yanking her fingernails out one by one," Stuart suggested, pretending to pull off his own fingernail. "They're probably working her over good so she won't dare bother you again."

A boy in a j.v. letter sweater ogled me. Aren't you the kid who came to school in a squad car? Nice going."

"Nice going?" I echoed. "Is he nuts?"

"Kobie, everybody thinks you're really cool now," Sandy said.

Mr. Grafius's door opened and Jeanette came out. Her eyes met mine. I doubted the vice-principals had "worked her over," but she must have gotten a pretty thorough talking-to. She didn't seem quite so sure of herself. A range of emotions flickered across her face: lingering anger, resentment, and, amazingly, grudging admiration. She stalked off without a word.

"Boy, is she ever impressed with you," Sandy said. For someone who had difficulty in math, Sandy could read people with uncanny accuracy.

Jeanette Adams impressed with me! Because I rode up in a squad car? Then it dawned on me that having to be dragged back to school by the law was an act of defiance that Jeanette would understand. Student beats system and all that. Going AWOL put me on a level with her and, in a perverse way, won her approval. She probably wouldn't pester me anymore. And even if she did, I could take care of myself, without muscle provided by the local police force. *This* freshman was tired of being intimidated.

The bell rang, and four thousand kids stampeded the halls. My mother was still with Miss Channing, listening to all the terrible things my teacher was telling her about me, so I had time to kill.

"I'll walk you guys to your bus," I offered.

Stuart climbed on his bus first. "See you tomorrow, Kobie. Maybe I'll have some of the money I owe you."

"I won't hold my breath," I said.

Sandy's bus was at the end of the line. "I think I'll make doughnuts tonight and bring them to school tomorrow. Just for you and me," she said.

My stomach rolled at the memory of our last batch of doughnuts.

"Hey, Kobie." Sandy put down the window next to her seat and stuck her head out. "Why don't we go shopping this weekend?"

Why not? There was certainly room in my life for a second best friend. Sandy was a troublemaker, but a well-meaning troublemaker. She had done lots of little things for me, like eat Jeanette's share of the banana cream pie, and defend my awful haircut, and stick up for me when Miss Channing gave me a failing grade Sandy thought I didn't deserve.

"Okay," I called up to her. "I want you to meet Gretchen, my other friend. We can all go together." I wondered if I should warn the stores that Sandy Robertson would be in the vicinity, in case they needed extra security.

I saw Marianne Andrews and Barbara Phillips get on the bus in front of Sandy's. They were laughing, as usual. I'd never noticed before that Marianne took such mincing little steps or how prissy Barbara was. Would Marianne have gone hunting for my dead body in the parking lot? Not very likely. If that wasn't a test of true friendship, I didn't know what was. Sandy and Stuart drove me crazy, but at least they weren't boring.

I didn't need Marianne or her group. I had my own group of friends, both at school and at home.

From where I stood I could see the roofline of Robert Frost Intermediate. The lunatic situation at Woodson probably would not improve, but I believed I could hold until the end of the year.

W.T. Woodson deserved another chance. And so did I. Maybe by the time I turned fifteen, I'd get it right.

For Kobie, making it to fifteen is a victory. After all, things are bound to get better — if she can stay out of trouble! Read more about the zany adventures of Kobie and her best friend Gretchen in FIFTEEN AT LAST, coming soon in Apple Paperbacks.

About the Author

CANDICE RANSOM, who is to this day amazed she made it through her freshman year, lives in Centreville, Virginia, with her husband and black cat. She writes books for young people and enjoys taking long walks through the woods near her home and browsing in antique and junk shops.